DOCTOR OF THE ISLES

Helen Murray

Curley Publishing, Inc.
South Yarmouth, Ma.

3 1336 02701 4605

Library of Congress Cataloging-in-Publication Data

Murray, Helen.
　　Doctor of the isles / Helen Murray—Large print ed.
　　　p. cm.
　　1. Large type books.　I. Title.
[PS3563.U769D6　1991]
813'.54—dc20
　ISBN 0–7927–0896–2 (lg. print)　　　　　　90–25855
　ISBN 0–7927–0897–0 (pbk: lg. print)　　　　　CIP

Copyright © 1971 by Donna Rix

All rights reserved. No part of this book may be used or reproduced in any manner without written permission except in the case of brief quotations embodied in critical articles and reviews.

Published in Large Print by arrangement with Dorchester Publishing, Inc. in the United States and Canada, the U.K. and British Commonwealth and the rest of the world market.

Distributed in Great Britain, Ireland and the Commonwealth by CHIVERS LIBRARY SERVICES LIMITED, Bath BA1 3HB, England.

Printed in Great Britain

DOCTOR OF THE ISLES

CHAPTER ONE

The powerful engine of the small seaplane roared echoingly across the glinting bay as it swooped down to kiss the smooth blue waters before settling to plough a creaming furrow across the surface. It headed in to the long, fingerlike landing stage poking out from the shore. Birds sailed up into the clear blue sky from their nearby nesting places in the rocky cliffs, disturbed by the discordant sound of engines. Diana Brett, squeezed into the narrow space beside the pilot, tightened her grip upon her medical bag and stared from the open cockpit, through the flying spray, at the group of natives waiting on the beach. Her long blonde hair was agitated by the slipstream, and she shrugged her slim shoulders inside her sticky white blouse as she prepared to land.

'That didn't take long, Doctor,' Jerry Todd commented as he craned his neck to watch the diminishing space between his craft and the end of the landing stage. His pale eyes showed even paler in the brilliance of the sunlight slashing at them from a faultlessly burnished sky, and his teeth glinted as he grinned. 'Have you many calls to make this afternoon?'

'Only three, Jerry,' Diana replied. She stifled a sigh, and her blue eyes were bright as she stared through narrowed lids at the sparkling water. 'I shall be ready to leave again in about thirty minutes.'

'I'll check the engine while I'm waiting for you. I noticed a faltering twice on the way over from St Flavia. We don't want to run the risk of ditching on the way back.'

'There's little fear of that with you as the pilot,' Diana said, pushing her hair back from her face. 'You live for this little craft of yours, Jerry.'

'That I do. I treat her as if she's human, and she's never let us down yet, has she?'

'Never, and I hope she'll never try.' Diana unfastened her safety belt and smoothed down her short white linen skirt. At thirty-two she was well set in her way of life as medical practitioner with an area of more than thirty thousand square miles to attend. Eight islands were located in the area, and she flew around her practice on strictly timed schedules, operating from the largest island of St Flavia, where her parents lived on a plantation. She suppressed a yawn as a grinning native on the end of the landing stage leaped upon the nearer float of the plane with a mooring rope in his hands, and the little craft rocked slightly under his moving weight. 'We'll be going on to Rango after this, then down to St Guill. If there are no emergencies we'll head back for St Flavia afterwards.'

'You'll be lucky if there are no emergencies,' Jerry Todd said, shaking his head as he cut the engine, and the echoes fled slowly and peacefulness returned as Diana opened her door and sprang lightly upon the landing stage.

She was tall and strikingly attractive, with a gentle face and small, regular features. Her complexion was dark from constant burning by the sun, and her teeth glinted remarkably by contrast when she smiled, which was often. She straightened her shoulders and took a tighter grip upon her bag, and as she stepped off the landing stage a group of dark skinned children came running about her, in high spirits because of her arrival. Diana knew them all and greeted them as friends, and they followed her up the cliff path and along to the collection of small buildings which formed their homes.

The island of Tope, some fifty-five miles from St Flavia, was set in the sparkling blue waters of the Caribbean like a tiny jewel shining remotely from its pale setting. One of seven isles forming a rough circle around the larger island of St Flavia, it was a lonely spot which boasted of nothing more than a temporary home for two dozen fishing families. A policeman posted on the island maintained a radio set which was the only link with headquarters, and it was his duty to report sickness among the few islanders in order that Diana could be informed. She was here now in response to a message, and her arrival was always a looked-for event among the children. Her progress around the island was heralded by the children, and their noise caused the native policeman to appear. He greeted Diana for the saviour she was, and conducted her to the patients who needed her attention.

With three cases only, Diana was soon on her way back to the landing stage, and she was followed by the children, still shouting and calling around her. She paused for a moment on the top of the cliffs and stared down into the bay. The seaplane looked like a large white seabird, nestling as it did in the anchorage, and a smile of pleasure touched her lips as she took in the peaceful scene. Farther out, the deeper waters of the open sea stretched away unbrokenly into the distance. A slowly moving boat caught Diana's gaze as it crept around a headland, and she watched it for a moment, trying to recognize it. In her four years as doctor to the Seaward

Islands she had come to know everyone and everything, but she hadn't seen this particular craft before, and that interested her.

The boat was dirty, as if it was nearing the end of a long, hard voyage, and it was quite large. Grey sails clawed what power they could from the fairly stiff breeze, and Diana saw that the craft was intending to fetch up alongside the landing stage. She glanced down at the seaplane again, and could make out the tiny figure of Jerry Todd upon it as he checked his precious engine.

She started down the path with the children at her heels, and by the time she reached the landing stage the boat was very close. Jerry was wiping his large, capable hands upon a piece of cotton waste, watching the newcomer also, and Diana paused at his side and remained silent as the boat came on over the last, intervening yards.

'Never seen this one before,' Jerry remarked. 'Stranger in these waters, and she's come a long way by the looks of her.'

'That's what I thought. Is it another trader?'

'Got that look about her, but I doubt it.' Jerry Todd was a short, grizzled man in his middle-fifties, with a wrinkled face that looked as if it had been cut from leather. His eyes shone startlingly blue from his creased countenance, and he was wiry, endowed with an inner vitality that made him seem like a man too tightly wound to sit still.

The sails on the straining mast suddenly began to furl, and Diana narrowed her eyes to make out some details of the figures on the deck of the craft. She saw a large man at the wheel aft, his chest straining at the grey singlet he was wearing, and his braced legs were encased in flannel trousers that had seen better times. A smaller man was being helped by a native to lower the sails, and Diana widened her eyes in surprise when she recognized the native as Polynesian. But it was the man standing in the bows of the boat, doing nothing to help the crew, who caught Diana's attention and held it.

He was tall and powerfully built, with a strangely intent face that held her eyes. His eyes were upon her now, and she felt the impact of their gaze as the boat came to stop at the landing stage with hardly a bump. The distance between them was barely ten yards, and the dark eyes of the stranger studied Diana with an intentness that disconcerted her, made her aware that her blouse was crumpled and limp from the heat and that her skirt was stained where she had slipped on the cliff path. But he was no better dressed, being bare above the waist, his torso gleaming brown and heavily muscled. He was wearing Bermuda shorts tightly belted at his surprisingly slim waist, and there was nothing on his feet. He placed a hand upon the rail of the boat and leapt lightly over it, dropping on his bare feet upon the landing stage with an impact that made it shudder. Diana found him towering head and shoulders above her, and she suddenly felt confused by his nearness.

'Hello,' he greeted in a rich-toned voice. 'Do you travel in the plane?'

'That's right,' Jerry said, grinning. 'Faster than your style.' He glanced at Diana, the sunlight making her eyes seem paler than ever. 'This is Doctor Brett, from St Flavia, and I'm Jerry Todd, her pilot.'

'How do you do?' The tones were studiedly casual. 'I'm Fenton Leigh, and this is my ship *Argo*. We're making for the island of St Lydia.'

'Ah!' Jerry Todd nodded his understanding. 'You must be the man they're all waiting for.' He half turned to Diana to explain. 'Remember the Leigh plantation on St Lydia?'

'It belonged to my father,' Fenton Leigh said. 'He died four months ago and I've come to take over the management.'

'Do you know anything about plantation

work?' Jerry demanded.

'I can soon learn.' There was deep conviction in the man's tones, and Diana found that his gaze did not leave her face. 'I have done many things in my time, and the climate here is little different to what I've been accustomed to.'

'You've come from the Pacific,' Jerry said.

'You seem to know a lot about me,' came the steady reply.

'I get around quite a lot, and in this job you get to know everyone and about everyone. But you've still got a couple of hundred miles to go to St Lydia. Having any trouble?'

'Not at all. We're merely taking our time.' Fenton Leigh's eyes were upon Diana all the time, and she suddenly found herself tongue-tied and unable to think clearly. He turned away and called over his shoulder to his crew, giving them sharp orders in a terse voice, and bare feet pattered upon the deck as they hurried to obey. When he turned back to look at Diana again she caught her breath at the power of his personality. He seemed to exude an aura of maleness that made itself obvious instantly, and she thought he was aware of it. She couldn't tell his age, although he would probably be around her own age. But he was a most compelling man, and he was making quite an impact upon her subconscious self, the very power of it filling her with instant disquiet.

'We'd better get along,' she said suddenly. 'We're a little pushed for time as it is. We've got two more islands to visit before we can return to St Flavia.'

'You attend all the islands in this group?' Leigh demanded.

'Yes.' Diana found it difficult to keep her tones level and casual. 'It's a demanding job, with very little free time. We work to tight schedules.'

'I see. Perhaps we shall see something of you on St Lydia then.'

'We call there several times a week.' Diana tightened her grip upon the medical bag, and Jerry grinned as he stepped on to the nearer float of the seaplane and prepared to take her hand.

Leigh took the medical bag from her and walked beside her as Diana boarded the plane. He grinned up at her when she was in the cockpit, and her hands trembled as she took the bag from him. He stepped back and saluted her, then turned and vaulted aboard his boat and stood watching her.

Diana tried to keep her eyes away from him while Jerry prepared for take-off, but her will power was not strong enough, and she finally gave up trying and let her gaze hold him. As the plane moved slowly away from the landing stage, accompanied by the powerful roaring of the engine, the crew on the boat crowded the rail and watched with lively interest. They waved as Jerry sent the plane away in a flurry of spray, and Diana turned her head to keep Fenton Leigh in sight until it was physically impossible to do so. At the last moment he lifted a hand and waved, and she waved in reply without realizing that she had done so. The next moment they were aloft and soaring high, and she twisted a little to stare down at the boat.

Jerry grinned at her and sent the plane around in a wide arc across the bay, one eye on the cliffs to the side and the other watching his instruments. It never ceased to amaze Diana how he could fly across the featureless seas and find their landfall with no problems at all. She knew nothing about navigating, beyond being aware that it was a precise science.

'Well, what do you make of Fenton Leigh?' Jerry demanded when they were flying smoothly in the direction of St Guill. 'He seems to be a strange one, doesn't he?'

'How do you mean?' Diana glanced at her companion with some interest, wondering if his impressions were the same as hers.

'He seemed more like a native himself, than

an Englishman. I have heard a lot about him. His father was a strange one, as you well know.'

'Yes, I attended him in his last illness.' Diana was casting her mind back into her case histories and trying to remember all she could about the Leigh family. There wasn't much to recall. She could remember the father, a tough old man of eighty-one when he had died four months previously, but she could not reconcile her memory of that man with the appearance of this strange son. There was considerable estate, she knew, and there had been a lot of talk about this missing son, who had not arrived even for his father's funeral. At first the lawyers hadn't been able to discover his whereabouts at all, and now four months had passed away and he had just arrived to collect his inheritance.

She fell to musing about Fenton Leigh. Her mind was eager to dwell upon him! That in itself was strange because she had a reputation on the islands for being a manhater, so much did she refrain from their company, but the truth of the matter was that medicine was her whole life and didn't leave anything over for anything else. The only man she did permit herself to go out with occasionally was Geoffrey Foster, her father's plantation manager. But they were only friends, and

Geoffrey had never ever attempted to kiss her. Romance was low on Diana's list of priorities. It had no part in her scheme of things.

They landed at St Guill and Diana attended four patients and inoculated all the children. They went on to Tara, now flying south and west of St Flavia, and after visiting Tara they turned north and flew back to St Flavia.

St Flavia appeared low on the horizon in the late afternoon sun, and Diana was somehow relieved to be at the end of her travelling for the day. She could not get her mind away from Fenton Leigh, and there was a frown on her lovely face when she finally alighted from the seaplane and prepared to go to the hospital standing on the top of the cliffs just outside the small township of Tenka. She paused until Jerry joined her on the landing stage, and her face was serious as she spoke to him.

'You'll be standing by in case of emergency, won't you?' she demanded.

'As usual.' He nodded and grinned. 'I'm going to try and find out a little more about Fenton Leigh. That man intrigued me, Doctor.'

She didn't admit that she, too, was intrigued by the stranger, and she had to resist the temptation to ask Jerry to let her know what he'd discovered. She shook her head slowly as she considered the fact, and she set out for the hospital with resolution in her stride, but she could not get her mind from that meeting with Fenton Leigh.

The hospital was Diana's headquarters, where all requests for a doctor were forwarded. She took clinics at the hospital, and had a surgery in the town itself for ordinary patients, although she lived in the large house on her father's plantation some miles out of town. She signed herself in and learned that there was no emergency to be considered, and she left her future whereabouts with the switchboard operator and prepared to go home. She would hold an evening surgery in town, but there was time enough for her to go home for a short rest before considering her last duties of the day. She was still very much pre-occupied as she drove herself out of town in her small yellow car.

The big white house on the hill overlooking the valley was clean looking in the sunlight, and sight of it never failed to make Diana's heart beat more quickly. She slowed the car to take her usual look at the valley, and she loved what she saw. The years she had spent in England during her studies and training had been difficult for her, having been born on the island, but both her parents were English, her father's family having lived in Kent for many years. But she looked upon herself as a native of St Flavia, and she had found England strangely foreign in many ways during her stay there. The weather had been dreadful all the time, and she had never become used to it. She was a tropical bird by heart and nature, completely happy here and satisfied with her simple way of life.

She left her car in the yard before the house and took her medical bag with her when she entered the house. The tall building had been built with comfort in mind, and the rooms were cool and roomy. Vinia Owen, the native housekeeper, appeared from the kitchen and called a cheery greeting. The woman was tall and lithe, and had been housekeeper for as long as Diana could remember. She was a widow, and her daughter Leona lived and worked in the house as a maid, but Leona was not like her mother and sulked a lot if she found too much to do. She was at an age where she liked to flaunt herself around the fields and flirt with the field-workers.

'Mrs Brett went into Tenka, Doctor,' Vinia said in her caressing voice. 'What have you had to eat today?'

'Nothing much, and I'm due to be in the town surgery in an hour and a half.'

'Go take a shower and rest yourself. I'll

have an iced drink waiting for you when you come down. Is there anything special I can get you to eat?'

'Nothing, thank you, Vinia. Where's Leona?'

'That girl!' There was mock disgust in the older woman's syrupy tones. 'I just don't know what to do with her, Doctor, and that's a fact. She's the plague of my life, and I don't get no answer when I ask the good Lord why she was thrust upon me.'

Diana smiled as she set down her bag and started up the stairs to her room. Vinia's husband had been drowned years before during a storm, when Leona had been but a child, but Vinia had made no secret of the fact that his going had been the blessing of the Lord, to whom she called loudly to stress every point she ever made. But Vinia had a heart of gold beating within her dusky body, and Diana had been feeling a little concerned about Leona lately because of the tales she'd heard. The girl was over eager to find love, and had made no secret of the fact. The natives on the island were like children in their recitals of doings among themselves, and although no one condemned Leona there was a great deal of shame for Vinia.

A shower and a change of clothing did much to refresh Diana, but nothing she did could erase the marks made in her mind by the meeting with Fenton Leigh. She went down to sit in the shade of the verandah, and Vinia brought her a tray and served iced drinks, but nothing could break the lock that the meeting seemed to have had in Diana's mind.

'Vinia,' she said slowly, 'what can you tell me about the Leigh estate on St Lydia?'

'I don't know much about them, Doctor. The old man died. You put him away. There are two sons, but no one has seen them both on the plantation yet.'

'Two sons! I thought there was only one!'

'Two sons! Twins.' Vinia chatted on, telling all she knew about the family, but Diana was hardly interested in more. She sat resting until it was time to take her surgery, and her mind was still filled with thoughts of Fenton Leigh when she drove into town.

She had several patients to see during evening surgery, and she dealt with them as quickly as possible, trying to keep her mind upon her work. When she rang the bell for another patient and her mother appeared, she knew her duties were at an end.

'There's no one else in the waiting room, Diana,' Lillian Brett said cheerfully. 'Does that mean you're through here for the day?'

'I hope so. It's been rather tiring today.'

Diana tried to keep her tones level as she studied her mother's smooth face. She found it hard to believe that her mother was fifty-four, because there seemed to be very little difference between them. Diana took after her mother. Both were tall and slim and blonde, and Diana was the only child, but despite that fact Lillian Brett was a most youthful looking person. They were very good friends as well as being mother and daughter. And Lillian made no secret of the fact that she was very proud of Diana.

'Has anything happened to upset you, dear?' Lillian studied Diana's face, and saw something of the strain working in her mind.

'I don't get upset by anything, and you well know it,' Diana said with a smile. 'No, nothing has upset me. It all went off as smoothly as always. With Jerry Todd as my pilot I never have any worries. What I shall do when he leaves I just don't know!'

'But surely all that trouble he was having is over and done with now!'

'I suspect it is, but Jerry isn't really happy any more since his wife left. He doesn't talk about her now, but I know it is on his mind at times.'

'He's such a cheerful fellow, and I feel quite secure when I know you're with him. What he doesn't know about flying isn't worth knowing.'

'He's supplanted his wife in his mind with that little seaplane,' Diana said warmly. 'He treats it as if it lived and breathed. I suppose it does for him!'

'Well if you're through here perhaps I can cadge a lift back home with you!' Lillian removed her white gloves and put them on Diana's desk. 'Father brought me in and left me, promising to come back later, but he telephoned the hotel to say he couldn't make it before seven-thirty. I want to be home before then because Mrs Reid is calling soon after, and I wouldn't want to miss her for anything.'

'Mrs Reid,' Diana said. 'That old busybody. It's scandalous how she talks about everyone. You ought to be ashamed of yourself for encouraging her, Mother!'

'She has her uses, Diana, so come along, if you're quite ready. Your days are quite long enough without you hanging back here.'

'I had a most unusual experience today,' Diana admitted as they walked to her car. She began to explain it, as she drove out of town, and Mrs. Brett was immediately interested. She heard Diana out, then cleared her throat excitedly.

'This is exciting news,' she said quickly.

'You obviously haven't heard the story of the Leigh twins, have you?'

'I didn't know there were twins until Vinia told me this afternoon!' Diana glanced at her mother with suddenly quickening senses. 'But what is so surprising about the arrival of Fenton Leigh?'

'He was disinherited by his father a few years ago as a thoroughly worthless lot, and his brother Willard has been expecting to inherit everything ever since. But from what Mrs Reid said the other evening Willard isn't getting even half the estate, and Fenton is supposed to be on his way here from wherever he's been hiding himself these past years. So you saw him at Tope! Well he will certainly enliven things around here. He was a doctor once, but got struck off, or whatever it is they call it when someone commits some crime or acts in a way not befitting a doctor. I don't know exactly what the trouble was, but they say Fenton Leigh is a very singular man, and I've been looking forward to meeting him. Tell me all about him, Diana, and don't overlook a thing.'

Diana told her mother something of her impressions, but could not begin to find the words necessary to explain the domination Fenton Leigh had secured over her mind. But she had thought his name familiar when

Jerry Todd first mentioned it. A chord had been struck in the back of her mind. His personality had forced the chord to remain unheard until now. Mrs Brett's mentioning that Fenton Leigh had been a doctor now cleared Diana's mind a little, and she grasped eagerly at the knowledge that came sweeping in.

Fenton Leigh had been struck off the roll because of conduct unbecoming a doctor. There had been a criminal charge laid against his name, a charge which had been proved against him. Diana narrowed her eyes as she recalled the newspaper reports she had read. Fenton Leigh had deliberately ended a patient's life because there had been, in his estimation, no hope and only suffering left. It had been a sensational trial at the time, although Diana herself had been busy in England with her own work. But she recalled it all so very clearly now, and she remembered that at the time she had felt a lot of sympathy for the unknown doctor who had dared follow the dictates of his own heart rather than the strict code laid down by his profession. So that was Fenton Leigh!

The knowledge only added to the growing confusion in her mind, and she could not help thinking that the future, with Fenton Leigh in the islands, would somehow take on a new meaning, and she was surprised to realize that she was already looking forward to meeting him again!

CHAPTER TWO

In the two days following that meeting with Fenton Leigh, Diana hoped for some reason to visit St Lydia, which lay about fifty-five miles to the south and west of St Flavia. Her great impatience troubled her, for she knew Fenton Leigh couldn't have reached home yet. He hadn't seemed in a great hurry that afternoon at Tope island. To her avid mind, it seemed that he was a man from another time; a more leisurely, uncomplicated period, and her short memory of him took on colours and impressions she knew were unreal. It also troubled her that he should have made such a lasting impression upon her usually sensible mind, but even the knowledge that he was an ex-doctor added to the interest he created inside her.

The two days were very busy for her as she flew among the islands on her cases. When, on the third day, she had to go to St Lydia, she began to tremble inside, for she sensed that she would see Fenton Leigh again. It was early in the morning when they left St Flavia, and Jerry Todd had the engine of the little seaplane tuned to a hair. The bright morning sun almost blinded Diana with its reflected glare from the smooth surface of quicksilver that was the sea. She liked the breeze in her face, for they sat in an open cockpit whenever possible, and Diana had unconsciously dressed for a possible meeting with the strange man who intrigued her.

Jerry touched down on the flat surface of a lagoon near the village that formed the centre of life upon the little island, and never had Diana's excitement been so intense. She had looked eagerly at the small natural harbour as they swooped over, but there had been no sign of Fenton Leigh's schooner. That fact could not detract from her enthusiasm, and she was wondering how to broach the subject of Fenton Leigh as Jerry helped her from the plane. But she needn't have worried. Jerry straightened his back as they stood for a moment on the landing stage, and as he looked around he caught Diana's eye.

'I wonder if Leigh got here from Tope, Doctor!'

'I've been wondering about him myself, Jerry. Didn't you find him an interesting person?'

'He struck me like that. I can't hardly explain it. He is different somehow.'

'That's the impression I got. But there's quite a story to him, I believe.'

'And one that should interest you,' the pilot retorted. 'He was stricken from the roll, so they tell me. He was a doctor who went wrong. You'd better be careful if you ever meet him again. He might lead you into bad ways.' He grinned as he spoke, and Diana shook her head and smiled.

'I'm going over to the Clinic first, Jerry, to find out what I've got this morning. I don't suppose we'll get away from here inside of two hours.'

'That's all right by me, Doctor. You go ahead and take all the time you need. I'll find something to occupy myself.'

She left him and walked into the village. The children came flocking around her, as usual, and she greeted them happily and they followed her to the tin hut Clinic, which was in the charge of a qualified native nurse. The nurse came to the door of the clinic, attracted by the noise of the children, and she greeted Diana warmly, her dark face wreathed in smiles.

'Hello, Doctor. I heard you coming. I have several patients for you this morning. You're right on time, as usual.'

'Punctuality is a fine thing, Maria,' Diana replied, shaking hands with the girl. 'How are the Thompson children?'

'Quite recovered now, Doctor. And Mrs Lang is comfortable. Perhaps you'll call on her if you have the time today.'

'I want to look in on her. But first let's look at the patients you have for me. Are they waiting?'

'All except one, but I expect he'll come now if he's heard the plane arrive.'

Diana nodded and went into her small surgery. The heat was vibrant under the tin roof, and she crossed to the open window and took a deep breath. Then she went to the battered old desk and sat down at it, opening her medical bag to check through its contents. Maria tapped at the door and entered, and Diana intimated that she was ready for the first patient.

She knew most of the islanders in the group! At one time or another during the four years that Diana had been their doctor, she had treated most of them, and they were the most friendly panel of patients she had ever known. The great majority of them were native, with a sprinkling of whites among them, and wherever she went, Diana was sure of a warm welcome by these open-hearted people. She attended their ailments and took care of their children, and they loved her for the care which she took. That morning she saw seven adults, and then checked the list of whites on the island needing her attention. She usually visited the whites at their homes, being driven in a Landrover by a habitually grinning native man who answered to the single name Tom!

'Tom cannot drive you today, Doctor,' Maria said when the last of the native patients had been attended to. 'He has gone to Tuna to visit his father. There is some family trouble, and Tom has to sort it out.'

'I see. Well perhaps I can get Jerry to drive me. I don't think he has much to do, unless he's tinkering with the plane again.'

'Here is the list of people who want to see you.' Maria held out a sheet of notepaper, and her dusky face was serious as she met Diana's gaze.

'Is there something worrying you, Maria?' Diana demanded. She knew this young woman intimately, and could tell by her expression that she was concerned about something. Maria took her work very seriously, and on more than one occasion her devotion and dedication had saved a patient's life. Diana knew that it must be a patient worrying the girl.

'I promised not to tell!'

'You made a promise to a patient?' Diana frowned, deciding it would be better to act the superior in order to draw the girl. 'I have told you never to do that, Maria.'

'But this man isn't a patient. He's the man I love, and I hope he will marry me.'

'I see. Well what's the trouble?'

'He has pains in the stomach and will not let me treat him. He is against seeing you, too!'

'What kind of pains are they? Have you been able to judge?'

'I think it is appendicitis! They are those pains. I would like you to see him, but he has threatened to forget me if I tell you about him.'

'Is he afraid?'

'He is like a child when it comes to medicine. He thinks if he can endure the pains long enough they will cease to bother him and go away.'

'But you know differently, don't you, Maria?' Diana nodded slowly. 'Where is this young man now?'

'He works on the Leigh plantation, and lives there in the workers' quarters.

Diana's heart seemed to miss a beat at the mention of the name. She took a deep breath and stifled a sigh, and a pang of excitement spread through her.

'What's his name, Maria? I'll call in there on my round and try to see him.'

'He is Andrew Griffith, Doctor, but if you see him I shall lose him.'

'I don't think so, Maria. If we can prove that he has nothing to worry about he'll thank you for helping him. If there is something wrong with him then the sooner we discover what it is the better.'

'I know that is right. Perhaps you would call to see him.' Maria's dark eyes were filled with agony. 'I would rather he turn away from me and live than die because of my love for him,' the girl said bravely.

'That's the spirit.' Diana patted her arm. 'But I don't think it will go to that extreme.' She glanced at the list the girl had given her. 'I'd better get a move on if I want to finish in time to go on to Tuna. I'm carrying out some tests on Tuna, Maria.'

'You are always doing a lot of good somewhere in the islands,' the girl responded.

Diana smiled and took her leave, and she hurried back to the landing stage where the seaplane rode at anchor. She found Jerry dozing in the shade of a nearby tree, and apologized as she shook him.

'Jerry, I know you deserve this rest, but I'm without a driver this morning and I need to get around the island. Will you drive the Landrover?'

'Certainly, Doctor. It will give me something to do. I need an occupation to enable me to keep my eyes open during the day.'

They walked back to the clinic, where the vehicle was garaged, and soon they were on their way. Diana arranged their route to take in the visits she needed to make with the minimum of travelling. But all the time she was thinking of the Leigh plantation, and she could hardly control her impatience to get there. The roads were dusty, but she didn't notice the discomforts this morning, and when she finally told Jerry to drive to the Leigh plantation she could hardly keep a quiver of emotion out of her tones. He glanced enquiringly at her as they changed direction, but said nothing, and Diana, afraid that he might be jumping to conclusions, hastened to explain the situation. But Jerry only nodded disinterestedly, and Diana lapsed into silence and struggled with her inner feelings as they neared their destination.

Jerry drove in through a gateway and went on towards the large white house standing among a dense grove of trees. It had been some months since Diana was last here, when the old man had died. She looked around eagerly now, to see what changes had taken place, and she was not surprised to see that a good many of the buildings had been repaired. Old Mr Leigh had let things slide a little, but his son Willard had remedied the faults in the past short time since his father's death.

'Up to the house, or shall we enquire of the manager?' Jerry slowed the Landrover and glanced at her.

'I suppose I'd better have a talk with the manager. He's Mr Anders, isn't he?'

'That's right. A very nice chap. He's the man to see all right.' Jerry drove to a smaller building apart from the rest of the plantation buildings, and Diana heaved a sigh as she climbed out of the vehicle. Jerry lounged in his seat and grinned at her as she caught his eye. 'Call me if you need anything,' he said, and tipped his battered old hat forward over his eyes.

Diana went to the front door of the bungalow and rapped on the fly screen, and within a moment or two the door was opened by a tall, middle-aged white woman. Diana hadn't met her before, but had heard that recently the Leigh plantation manager had fetched himself a new wife from England.

'I'm Doctor Brett,' Diana said slowly. 'You must be Mrs Anders.'

'That's right, Doctor.' The woman smiled a

welcome. 'I've heard all about you, and I've been waiting for the opportunity to meet you. Please come in. What can I do for you?'

Diana entered the bungalow and set down her bag. She explained the reason for her visit.

'We must certainly look into this,' Mrs Anders said, nodding emphatically. 'I've only been here a short time, as you probably know, Doctor, but I do so want to help where I can, and I think I can best help by taking an interest in the welfare of the workers.' She paused and excused herself, and walked to the door before halting and facing Diana. 'I'll send my servant to find my husband and ask him to bring the worker here. Will you have an iced drink, Doctor, or some coffee? You look hot and tired.'

'I'd like coffee, please, Mrs Anders. This is a very comfortable room.'

'I haven't done everything I want to do yet,' the woman replied happily. 'Bob lived here alone before we were married, and you can imagine the kind of home a bachelor keeps. But it is slowly coming around to my liking. What was the name of that worker again, Doctor?'

'Andrew Griffith!' Diana relaxed as Mrs Anders departed, and she looked around the room and saw the improvements that only a woman's hand could make. She felt that Bob Anders was a very lucky man.

Mrs Anders returned shortly, a smile on her homely face. She was in her late forties, perhaps a little older, Diana judged, and already she was hungry for female companionship. They chatted about general things until their coffee was served and afterwards Diana asked the usual questions that one demanded of a newcomer to the islands.

'I think this is a wonderful place, and my only regret is that I didn't come out years before,' Mrs Anders said enthusiastically. 'I don't think I shall ever get used to the exotic nature of everything. This is a totally different world to the one I'm accustomed to. But I wouldn't want to go back to England, not even for a holiday.'

'Mr Anders has been out here for a number of years, hasn't he?'

'Yes. About ten years. I knew Bob when we were both in our teens, and he wanted to marry me before he came out here. But I had a widowed mother who wasn't in the best of health, so I stayed behind. She died a few months ago, and when I had tidied up my affairs in England I came straight out here. I haven't looked back since.'

'I hope you'll continue to be happy here,

Mrs Anders,' Diana said.

There was a short silence, and Diana felt the desire to change the subject. She wanted to ask questions about the Leighs, but wondered how to broach the subject. Finally her curiosity could not be contained longer, and she took a deep breath and tried to make her voice sound casual as she spoke.

'Three days ago I was on the island of Tope, visiting some patients,' she said. 'A schooner entered the bay just before we left,' She went on to tell Mrs Anders about her meeting with Fenton Leigh, and the woman's dark eyes glowed a little with interest.

'Fenton arrived here yesterday evening,' she said, 'I had met Willard, and I was struck by his personality. He is certainly the most male man I've ever come into contact with. It seems to leap at you when you get within feet of him. But when I met Fenton last evening it was like running into an electric cable. I was staggered, and when he shook hands it was like getting burned. He seems to overwhelm a mere woman! But by his appearance one would judge him as a masterful man, someone who thinks of himself as a force to be reckoned with.' Mrs Anders paused and smiled. 'I don't know if this exotic place has charged my mind with romance, but I could imagine Fenton Leigh as a pirate Captain in another age; not one of those cut-throat villains, but of the type one sees portrayed in films. Yet, speaking to him last evening, I discovered that he's not at all as his image suggests. He's very quiet and aloof, and it was hard to keep him talking.'

'I found him a bit of a surprise when I met him,' Diana admitted.

'He did mention you, as a matter of fact,' Mrs Anders said. She smiled as she looked into Diana's blue eyes. 'I got the feeling that you made quite an impact on him!'

Diana began to feel uncomfortable under the woman's gaze, and she was quite relieved when the door of the room was suddenly opened and Bob Anders entered.

'Hello, Doctor,' he greeted, coming forward with outstretched hand. 'It's nice to see you again. I've been meaning to get in touch with you. I thought it would be nice if you and Melanie got to know each other. But you'll be wanting to see your patient, no doubt. I've brought him along. He was complaining two days ago of pains in the stomach, but he wouldn't report sick. I've put him in my study. You can examine him there if you wish. There is a couch in the room.'

'Thank you, Mr Anders.' Diana got to her feet.

'Are you in a hurry to leave when you're

through here?' he demanded, showing her out of the room and along to his study.

'Not particularly, although I have to go on to Tuna. Is there something you want?'

'Not something I want, but one of the bosses returned home yesterday, and he was talking about you. He met you on Tope a few days ago.'

'Fenton Leigh!' Diana caught her breath. 'Yes, Mrs Anders was talking about him a few moments ago. Is he settling here on St Lydia now?'

'I think so. He's going to take a hand in running the plantation, so he says. But he doesn't get along at all well with Willard.'

'I don't think that is so very surprising,' she remarked.

'Perhaps you're right. But if you have a few moments to spare I'd take you over to the house so Fenton can talk to you again.'

Diana's pulses raced at the thought, but she kept her face expressionless as they paused at the door of the study. Anders opened the door for her and she looked into the small room and saw a native youth standing by the window. He started visibly at sight of her, and his scared glance dropped to the medical bag she was carrying. Before they could say anything he had slipped out through the open window and was running fast across the wide yard. Anders muttered something under his breath and darted in pursuit, climbing through the window and chasing across the yard, calling out to the youth in loud tones that were meant to reassure him.

Diana shook her head as she watched and, when the youth disappeared from sight with Anders slowly gaining on him, she resigned herself to a longish wait and returned to the lounge, where Mrs Anders was waiting. Explaining the situation, Diana accepted another coffee, and they sat chatting until, some minutes later, Bob Anders returned with the youth, an arm on the fellow's shoulder.

'There you are,' Anders said as he escorted Andrew Griffith into the room. 'You know Doctor Brett very well. She has never hurt anyone in all the time I've known her, and she only wants to have a look at you. She isn't going to cut you open, or anything like that.'

Diana went forward and took the youth's arm. 'You mustn't be afraid, Andrew,' she said in kindly tones. 'If you have a pain then it should be investigated. Let us go into Mr Anders' study and you can tell me all about it.'

'Maria told you about me!' he accused, trembling as Diana led him to the door.

'Maria is a very sensible girl, and she knows

you probably need help. You're not afraid of me, are you?'

Anders followed them into the study, and he stood by the door while Diana made Griffith sit down on the couch. She asked questions about the youth's condition, trying hard to gain his confidence, and he slowly began to talk. From what he said Diana was fairly certain that he had acute appendicitis, and she tried to get him to lie down in order to examine him. He refused adamantly, but finally agreed to let Diana probe his abdomen. His dark eyes were large and frightened as he stared rigidly at her. Diana immediately discovered the area troubling him. She took his pulse and checked his temperature. His tongue was thickly coated, and Diana nodded slowly.

'Andrew, I know what your trouble is,' she said. 'I want you to go to St Flavia in the seaplane. You'll go into hospital for a few days.'

'I don't want to go to hospital. They'll cut me open,' he said.

'Perhaps not!' Diana stared into his frightened face. 'I am telling you the truth. If you go into hospital now they may be able to prevent this illness reaching the climax. I don't think it is too late. They would make you lie in bed and rest, and give you special food. If you don't go then this will slowly get worse, and you may die.'

He stared at her for some moments, indecision showing in his face and eyes, and Diana put a hand upon his shoulder.

'Don't be afraid,' she said gently. 'If you have to have the operation you wouldn't feel anything. You would go to sleep for a little while, and when you awoke again it would be all over. I think you would enjoy the trip in the seaplane, too.'

Anders joined in the conversation, trying to make the youth see sense, and slowly they managed to overcome his fears. They went out to the Landrover, where Jerry sat dozing. Diana gave the pilot instructions, for there wasn't enough room in the plane for the three of them, and Jerry would have to take Griffith to St Flavia, then come back for Diana.

The Landrover departed, and Diana heaved a sigh of relief.

'What a lot of patience you have, Doctor!' Anders said. 'But did you tell him the truth? Will he have to have an operation?'

'He most certainly will, and as soon as possible. I don't know how long the inflammation has been present in the appendix, but he will be relieved of it within the next twenty-four hours.'

'Let's hope Todd gets him to the hospital in

time,' Anders said. 'But you're at a loose end now, Doctor, and if I don't take you across to the house then I'll likely lose my job here. Fenton Leigh was wondering last night how he could meet you again, and here you are sitting on his doorstep with time to kill! To me, that smacks of the hand of Fate!'

Diana mentally agreed, and she wondered exactly what lay in store for her in the future, among all the as yet untouched days awaiting her. Dare she hope that Fenton Leigh would figure prominently among them? It was no surprise to her to realize that she hoped he would!

CHAPTER THREE

Diana was aware of her crumpled skirt and blouse as she walked across to the large house at Bob Anders' side. She was quivering inside, and despite her efforts to control the unusual emotions, she was uneasy and very excited as they reached the verandah. A man was sitting in a wicker chair on the verandah, with a small table at his side containing a tray of drinks. He got to his feet immediately he saw them, and Diana felt her heart lurch as she stared at him. But it wasn't Fenton Leigh, although her eyes tried to inform her that he was. This was Willard Leigh, a milder replica of his brother. Diana had seen him once or twice, but even during his father's last illness he hadn't shown himself to her, being content to rely upon his servants to get what information he required about his father. There had been rumours circulating the island about the Leigh family for as long as Diana could remember, most of them good, but there had been a slight air of mystery about these twin sons, and Diana had never known Fenton at all and Willard mainly by sight.

'Doctor Brett,' Willard Leigh said steadily. 'You haven't been here for some months.'

'I'm glad you've been enjoying good health,' she replied.

Bob Anders explained the situation, and Diana stood silently at his side, undergoing a very close scrutiny by Willard Leigh. He was like his brother, she was thinking, a little intense, but not nearly so powerful a personality. But for all that he was a strikingly handsome man, and now Diana was wondering why it was he had never found a bride among the many eager girls of the islands.

'You must certainly stay here with us until

your pilot returns, Doctor,' Willard said gallantly. He looked very cool, dressed in lightweight trousers and a pale blue silk shirt. His dark eyes were gleaming in his brown face, and he looked the healthy outdoor type that he was. His arms were muscular, shining with fine black hairs that greedily covered his flesh, even to the point of bunching thickly upon the backs of his strong fingers. 'We must summon Fenton and let him know that you're here. He was asking a lot of questions about you last evening. I understand that you met him on Tope the other day.'

'That's right.' Diana narrowed her blue eyes as she recalled that never to be forgotten afternoon! Her breath seemed to catch in her throat. She looked at Bob Anders as he prepared to depart, and she struggled to retain her composure. But Anders was smiling. 'Thank you for your help with Andrew Griffith, Mr Anders,' she hurried on. 'I'm sure we're saving his life by getting him off to hospital.'

'Perhaps you'll let me know what progress he makes,' Anders replied. 'But now I'd better get back to my work. Perhaps you will be calling on my wife again soon, Doctor.'

'I'll make a point of it,' Diana promised. 'I'm sure she must be feeling a little lonely with you at work all day.'

'Thank you, I'll tell her to watch out for you in a few days.' Anders nodded and departed, and Diana watched him as he crossed the yard.

'He's a good man,' Willard Leigh said slowly. 'I don't know where I would be without him. He was getting a bit restless before he married, but now Mrs Anders is with him he's settled down again.'

'I'm glad to hear that.' Diana returned her attention to his dark face, and a thrill travelled through her when she saw how closely he resembled his brother.

'Please sit down,' he said graciously, waving a hand towards the verandah lounge. 'What would you like to drink? It's all very fresh, and still cold.'

'Perhaps an orange juice,' Diana told him, and he moved to the table and prepared the drink for her. 'Thank you.' She tried not to tremble when their hands touched as she took the glass. But it was her thoughts of his brother, and not his own personality that was affecting her.

'If you'll excuse me for a moment I'll call Fenton,' he said. 'He would never forgive me if I let you go again without letting him know of your presence. What did you think of Fenton when you met him?'

'He's a little overwhelming,' she said cautiously, 'but a very nice person, I would say.'

'You're being cautious,' he accused with a smile. 'Fenton has always had a devastating effect upon women, and I can see by your expression that he made quite an impression on you.'

Diana made no reply, but she felt confused as he entered the house by way of french windows at the back of the verandah. She heard him calling, and she tried desperately hard to still her suddenly fast beating heart when she heard voices inside the room. A moment later Willard appeared again, and Fenton was at his side.

'You've already met Fenton,' Willard said smoothly, 'so there is no need for me to introduce you. I'll leave you in Fenton's hands, Doctor Brett. I have some work to attend to, if you'll excuse me. Fenton has nothing at all to do. He won't put on the harness for a week or two yet.'

Diana nodded, her eyes upon Fenton's strong, tanned face, and Willard took his leave, going almost without her noticing his departure. Fenton came forward and took her hands in his.

'So we meet again, Doctor!' he said softly. 'I was hoping we would. Let us sit down, and you can tell me all about your work around the islands.'

They sat down, and he chose the chair his brother had vacated. Diana felt like a small girl facing the headmaster for some slight misdemeanour, and she tried hard to dispel the illusion and act naturally.

'I'm sure you must know a great deal about my work hereabouts, Mr Leigh,' she replied. 'You were a doctor once, were you not?'

'So that hasn't been forgotten yet!' His face hardened for a moment, and his dark eyes registered sadness. Diana felt a pang stab through her, and she coloured slightly.

'I'm sorry! Perhaps I shouldn't have mentioned it, but being a doctor myself, I am quite interested in other doctors.'

'I'm no longer a doctor, and I left the islands a few years ago to try and forget what happened here. I know now that I shall never completely forget it, and people have proved that they don't easily forget either.'

'I didn't mean anything,' Diana said. 'I remember reading all about it, although I was studying in England then. I had quite a lot of sympathy for you, I remember.'

'Thank you. I believe there was considerable sympathy for me, but it didn't alter the facts, and now I'm trying to forget that rather painful episode.'

'You've been in the Pacific, haven't you?' Diana was eager to change the subject. 'I should like to hear you talk of those islands.'

'You'd be surprised to learn that there's very little difference between the islands there and these where you work.' He leaned forward and studied her face intently. 'What made you take up medicine, Doctor, and why did you settle for such a tough life as this one you're leading?'

'It isn't so very tough,' she disagreed lightly. 'I admit that I work a great many hours, and I have little free time, but I love my work and I wouldn't want to change this for anything else in the world.'

He smiled at her enthusiasm, and she watched his face closely. Her first impressions of him were being borne out, although this morning he didn't look so much a beachcomber, dressed as he was in neatly pressed flannels and a white nylon shirt. He was clean shaven and fresh looking now, with his hair neatly trimmed and his manner quite civilized. The other afternoon, standing as he had upon the deck of his schooner, he had seemed quite a different person. He was still a most attractive man, and his clothes and quiet, sober manner could not quite hide the real man beneath the sophisticated surface.

'Willard tells me that you nursed our father

through his last illness, until his death!'

'I did!' Diana leaned forward and looked earnestly into his face. 'He died peacefully. He wasn't in any pain. His illness lasted several weeks, but he was quite comfortable.'

'My lasting regret was that I didn't know of this until it was too late,' he said, shaking his head, and his eyes were bright with emotion. 'I left home because of the ruination of my career, as no doubt you are aware, and I didn't come back again until now. When I learned of my father's death something seemed to die inside me. I left home thinking it was better that I cut all ties, but when it was too late I realized that I should have stayed and tried to live it down. I wish I could have had some time with my father before he died. But thank you for what you did. Willard said he couldn't have been better treated.'

Diana remained silent, watching his face, and he stared at her for a few moments. The silence that developed between them wasn't at all awkward, and Diana was gaining the impression that she had known this man for a very long time. There didn't seem to be any strangeness between them. He had the ability of appearing like a friend of long standing! Diana, who had never found the habit of making friends easy, was astounded by the way she seemed to accept him.

'You're going to be here with me for quite some time,' he said at length. 'Did you have any more calls to make today?'

'No. I left this one until last. I have nothing to do until my pilot returns.'

'Then would you care to come for a walk with me? My ship is anchored in the bay just beyond that ridge. I think we have time to walk across there and back before you can reasonably expect your pilot to return.'

'I'd like to look over your ship, if I may,' Diana said boldly, and he nodded.

'I'll leave a message of your whereabouts, in case you are needed while we're away. They can easily send someone to fetch you.'

She watched him as he got to his feet, and he moved in a deliberate manner that seemed to hint at hidden reserves coiled in his powerful body. A trickle of undefinable desire shivered through Diana, and she tried to suppress it instantly. What was happening in her mind? The thought startled her. Here she was secretly attracted to a man she didn't know. She had been in his company for a total of only a few minutes, and yet he had aroused in her more interest and wonder than any man she had ever known. She had even forgotten about her work, so great an absorption his personality demanded!

He came back presently and she got to her

feet. They left the house and crossed the yard, passing through a gateway and finding a narrow path leading through the trees. The path climbed precipitously until they came breathlessly upon the top of the ridge, and there they paused to regain their breath, and Diana found before her a long slope that was thickly wooded. The trees seemed to go right down to the water's edge, but there was a thin white strip of sand marking the demarcation line between earth and sea.

Diana caught her breath at sight of his schooner riding peacefully at anchor in the calm waters of the little bay, and she was reminded of the first moment she had seen the craft. She turned and looked into his face, and found, to her surprise, that he was watching her closely. She started, and her expression softened a little. She moistened her lips, not realizing that she was adding to the allurement reaching out from her, and he moved impatiently and reached out and took hold of her arms. She tremored at his touch and he stared down into her face as he drew her close to him.

'You too!' he said. 'You feel drawn to me, don't you?' He smiled thinly as she nodded slowly. 'I've always been at a disadvantage because of it. I've always had a train of girls in my wake. Not that I'm the kind of man to indulge in that sort of thing. Being a doctor, you know how one's time is limited for personal things. It proved to be a nuisance where women patients were concerned. But you're different, Doctor Brett. The first moment I saw you standing there beside the seaplane I told myself that there was a girl in ten million. I thought I was dreaming at first. But you are real, and I'm glad that I've come back to these islands. You're not going to spoil everything now by telling me there is a man in your life, are you?'

He reached out and took hold of her long blonde hair, tugging it impishly as he looked down into her face, and he smiled as she smiled.

'I never have time for personal things,' she said slowly, her eyes narrowed against the glare of the sun coming down at them through the branches of the tree under which they were standing.

'So there's no one!' Relief shone in his dark eyes and showed plainly upon his face. 'Well I'm going to change all that, Diana.'

She started at the sound of her name upon his lips, and her mind was wavering under the pressures increasing inside her. He was still drawing her unprotestingly into his arms, and he leaned his broad shoulders back against the tree and stared hungrily into her face.

'Such a beautiful woman,' he said. 'For weeks I've had the feeling that something good at last was going to happen to me. I knew on Tope that you were that good thing. I could tell by your face that you were struck by me, and that sort of thing only happens once in a lifetime. Don't deny it.' He spoke quickly, as if afraid that she would speak out against his idea. 'Just relax and let Fate handle its own work.'

Diana found herself pressed against his powerful chest, his arms about her like steel bands, and the strength he possessed startled her for she was helpless against it. But what was most surprising was the fact that she did not want to protest at this surprising treatment. Deep inside, where her primeval urges lurked, she knew she had wanted to be kissed by him from the very first moment. Now she took the initiative, and lifted her arms to wind them tightly around his neck. He grunted with pleasure and held her even more tightly, and Diana closed her eyes and tilted her face, not caring that this definitely was not the correct behaviour for a qualified doctor. But she was being subjected to urges far beyond her control, and she knew instinctively, as his mouth came crushing down upon her own, that this was real and lasting.

Her senses seemed to shimmer and fade under the powerful emotions loosed inside her. She had never been in love in her life, but these feelings had nothing to do with pure love, with lighthearted romance. These emotions were part and parcel of life itself, a convulsive desire that was instinctive in men and women to find a mate and justify existence.

She clung to him as if her very life depended upon their contact. Her inhibitions, formed by a lifetime of social living and by the strict code of her profession, fled wildly before the onset of savage desire, and he held her so tightly that her heart seemed to stop beating. She became breathless, and wrenched herself free from him and laid her head against his powerful shoulder and gasped for breath. Her hair was down across her face, and he still held her, but gently. She closed her eyes, feeling that this was just some glorious dream born of her inner frustrations. By degrees her breathing returned to normal, and she lifted her head and looked into his expressionless face.

There was no need of words. They just stared at one another, and she could see herself in his dark eyes. Her hands rested lightly against his shoulders, and she was aware that they were still very close together.

'That was madness,' she whispered, and her throat was too constricted by what had passed to permit her vocal power.

'Is that what you would call it?' he demanded tensely. 'How can it be madness? It was a coming together of two souls intended to meet. Can't you feel that?'

'I can't feel anything at the moment. You've completely bludgeoned my senses.'

'But you wanted me to kiss you even before I put my hands upon you. I could see it in your eyes. You felt the same way I did. But do you think it was just a spontaneous reaction? Do you think it couldn't strike fire again, as it did just now?'

'I don't know!' She spoke in low, vibrant tones, and her eyes were alight with emotion.

'There's only one way to find out. Do I have your permission this time?'

'Yes.' The word was husky in her throat, and he pulled her to him again, his face suddenly sharp and tense. She went into his arms without protest, and he kissed her long and powerfully. Diana felt as if she had boarded a magic carpet and was being wafted up beyond the clouds to that mysterious land of love that few ever reached on earth. She had never been so moved before in her entire life, and she had a strange feeling that this moment ought to last forever.

When he released her his arms fell limply to his sides and he watched her. She remained close to him, her eyes wide as she stared into his face. Her hands were pressed against his chest, and she could feel the rise and fall of his lungs, the fast, powerful beating of his heart. A muscle twitched in his cheek, and there was sudden sadness in his eyes.

'What have I done to you?' he demanded. 'Have I filled you with desire? Where are your thoughts of duty?' He sighed heavily. 'I can see nothing in your eyes but the need for more of the same. You've been a lonely woman, Diana, going about your practice with your own hopes held prisoner. I know exactly how you've felt because I've suffered in the same way. But you've never been aware of the fact that somewhere in this wide world there was a man made especially for you!' His teeth glinted momentarily. 'But you know it now, don't you?'

She nodded slowly, aware that her will-power was gone completely. What kind of magic he wielded she did not know, but she was certain that no other man could have moved her as he did. She was trembling inside, filled with so many impressions and emotions that her mind could hardly cope with them all. She felt weak, and slightly embarrassed now, and she stared into his face, trying to regain her peace of mind.

'Shall we go down to the ship now?' he demanded.

She nodded, almost incapable of speech, and he took her arm and led her down the steep path through the trees. Diana tried to regain her composure as they made the descent, but by the time they reached the sand she was still feeling tremendously moved by their contact, and he looked down into her face and smiled gently.

'There are signals in your eyes and on your face,' he remarked.

'What are they saying?' she prompted.

'Do it again. Thrill me!'

'I don't understand you!' She looked at him squarely. 'Do you have a chip on your shoulder about women? Do you go around causing this mental upheaval for the purpose?'

'It may seem like that to you, but it isn't the case. I have never been married, or engaged, or really in love. I have never had a steady girl friend. Romance has always passed me by, although I have been chased by a few girls. But until now I have never willingly tried to attract a girl.'

'I'm the first one?' Diana stared at him, still grappling with her emotions.

'The very first and the last, I should imagine.' He took her arm again and led her across the sand to where a dinghy lay upon the shore.

She watched him push it into the water, noting the powerful bunching of his muscles, and he held it still while she stepped in. Then he pushed off and hopped into the boat without getting his feet wet. He took the oars and rowed out to the waiting schooner only fifty yards out, and he sent the dinghy thrusting through the water with his powerful strokes. In no time they were nosing against the larger ship, and Diana waited while he moored the dinghy. Then he leaped upwards and secured a hold on the ship's rail, pulling himself up, then reaching down for her hand. Diana trembled at his touch, and he lifted her easily and quickly to the deck of the ship.

The Polynesian was sitting on a coil of rope in the shade, asleep, completely relaxed, and Fenton grinned as they walked by on the way to the saloon. He descended the companionway ahead of Diana, and she followed quickly. He fetched drinks for them, and afterwards showed her over the ship. Diana lost all track of time, and as they looked around the ship he told her about the Pacific islands. She listened closely, taking in every word he said, and by the time they had completed a tour of the ship she was certain it was time to return to the shore.

'This has been a very diverting morning, Fenton!' she exclaimed as they walked back over the ridge to the house.

'I'm sure it's been a great experience for you.' His teeth glinted. 'But I suppose you're telling yourself right now that this is the last time you'll see me.'

'No!' She shook her head as she looked at him. 'Nothing is further from my thoughts.' She paused and considered for a moment. 'Unless you have been playing a game this morning just to amuse yourself, and what happened between us doesn't really matter!'

'Don't ever think that!' He paused and took her by the shoulders, gripping her a little so that his hands hurt. She set her teeth into her bottom lip, and he laughed softly and swept her into his arms. 'I've loved you for years,' he said. 'I've seen your face in every good dream I've ever had. But until the other afternoon you lived only in my mind. I have never even caught a glimpse of you or anyone coming anywhere near to you. But now you are here in the flesh, and you're never going to get away from me. Remember that, Diana Brett, good woman that you are. I'm in love with you and I know that we have a Fate to meet!'

'You're a strange man!' She shook her head wonderingly.

'No,' he rapped. 'Not at all strange! Honest, perhaps! But there are all too few honest people around!' He pulled her gently towards him and kissed her, this time exerting no power, and still Diana felt as if her senses were being stolen. 'I shall hope to see you again, and very soon,' he said, releasing her. His eyes lifted from her face and he stared down into the yard in front of the house. 'There's your pilot back for you. I suppose you'll have to go now.'

'My duties!' She shrugged a shoulder. 'I don't get to St Lydia very often. I don't know when I shall be able to see you again, Fenton.'

'You'll make the opportunity. You'll come back, or I shall come to St Flavia to see you. Now run along and get back to reality. I'm going back to my ship.'

'Goodbye,' Diana said breathlessly, and he smiled and turned away, walking back swiftly the way they had come. She stood watching his powerful figure until he was out of sight, and then a sigh escaped her and she let her shoulders slump a little. Her eyes narrowed as she walked down to the yard, and she could see Jerry Todd sitting in the Landrover in front of the house. She breathed deeply and tried to rid her mind of the sense of unreality, but it clung to her like the shadows hanging underneath the trees, and she felt that somewhere inside her there were important changes taking place. She had a vague idea that life would never be the same again!

CHAPTER FOUR

In the days that followed, Diana found it difficult to accept what had happened on St Lydia with Fenton Leigh. She had never felt the need of a man at any time in her adult life, and none had attracted her at all. But Fenton Leigh was in a class by himself, and she felt slightly ashamed that she had fallen victim of his appeal. But she could not forget the pleasure she had received in his arms, and there was a nagging insistence in her mind that warned her she would have trouble trying to forget him. That he had been amusing himself at her expense seemed fairly obvious to her in retrospect. But she didn't like the thought. His general manner seemed to inform her that he was not that sort of a man. But he had said many things that did not seem in character, and she was confused and unsettled by thoughts of him.

As the days went by she began to experience

a desire to see him again. At first she mastered it and thrust it away, for the pressures of her work were great, but each passing day added to the power of the desire, and she began to hope for a call to the island. She wanted to use the condition of Andrew Griffith as an excuse, but the native youth was operated on and made a fine recovery.

When she was off duty, Diana began to feel ill at ease, and on more than one occasion she walked along the shore of the island, to stand and stare across the sea in the direction of St Lydia, fifty-odd miles away, and she was not above dreaming and hoping that the schooner would suddenly appear on the horizon and come straight to her.

She had been in the habit of spending some of her off-duty time with Geoffrey Foster, her father's plantation manager. Geoffrey had come out from England five years before with a string of qualifications after his name, and he had proved in the following time that he was a useful man about the plantation. He was about thirty-three, a tall, slim, brown-eyed man of quiet manner, and he made no secret of the fact that he cared considerably for Diana. She had never encouraged him, but had needed a friend and he seemed to fit the bill. As the days went by and she made no effort to spend time with Geoffrey, he sought her out, and on the shore one evening, when Diana was seated on the warm sand and staring pensively across the sea, Geoffrey came from the trees and stood over her.

Diana didn't see him at first, so deep were her thoughts, and it wasn't until he spoke that she realized she was not alone.

'Diana, is there something wrong?' His face showed great concern as he squatted beside her, and she looked up into his dark eyes and shook her head.

'Wrong?' she demanded. 'What could possibly be wrong in this paradise?'

'You've been acting strangely for almost a week now. I've noticed it, and your parents are beginning to notice it. Is there something wrong with your work?'

'Good Heavens, no! What gave you that idea?' There was genuine surprise in Diana's face.

'You're so different, and you haven't attempted to see me in the evenings you've been free from duty. At one time you were always demanding to be taken for a walk along the shore, but I've been watching you and just lately you've done nothing but sit in this exact spot and stare out across the sea. What's the attraction on St Lydia?'

'St Lydia?'

'Yes. It lies in that direction.'

'So it does! But that has nothing to do with it. I just like this spot. I work rather hard, Geoffrey, and I'm entitled to a little solitude. It's good for the soul, didn't you know?'

'A little, yes. But you're spending every available moment out here. Your mother feels there's something worrying you.'

'Mothers are entitled to worry about their daughters.' Diana smiled a little. 'But I'm not a teenage girl to be worried over, Geoffrey. I'm an adult woman, and I do a very responsible job.'

'I wouldn't argue with that.' He sat down on the sand and wrapped his arms around his updrawn knees. 'I worry about you, Diana. I think you work too hard. Surely they could put another doctor on this practice. There must be enough work for two.'

'I expect there is, but I've got in the habit of doing everything for myself, and it isn't too difficult. I do plenty of flying, and I would work as many hours if I had a post at the hospital, you know.'

'Diana, there's quite a lot I want to talk over with you.' His tone changed, turned huskier, and she frowned as she glanced at him. He was a handsome man, and she knew several single girls on the island who looked upon him as a good catch. But Geoffrey had thrown himself into his work, and apart from

Diana herself he didn't look at a woman.

'Well this is as good a time and place as any,' she said. Then she tensed a little as her mind went to work and produced the subject most likely to be broached. She cringed inwardly, for she wanted to hear nothing of love and romance.

'I've known you for a number of years now,' he said slowly. 'In that time you haven't given a thought to any man, and I've never looked at another woman. I fell in love with you a long time ago and I've been trying to talk to you about it for so long that it's become an obsession to me. But I cannot wait any longer, Diana! I want you to know that I love you, and I hope you have some feelings for me!'

She caught her breath for a moment as the import of his words sank in. Their eyes met and Diana could see the deadly seriousness in him. But she shook her head slowly. Somehow, his words came as no great surprise.

'Geoffrey, I don't know what to say!' she told him.

'I expect this has come as a surprise.' His awkwardness vanished as he warmed to the subject. 'But I feel that we've become very close since I've been in the islands. Your mother was saying that if you didn't fall in love with me then you'd never fall in love.'

'You've been discussing me with my mother?' she demanded.

'I did ask her what she thought my chances were!'

'I see!' Diana shook her head. 'Well I'd better make my feelings clear. I'm not in love with you, Geoffrey, and I don't suppose I ever shall be. It would have shown itself by now if it was going to happen. I'm totally in love with my work. I've never even considered love and marriage. Some women are not born to it, and I'm certain to be one of them.'

'You think that way because you've never considered it,' he retorted. 'Please consider it now, Diana. Let it run through your mind for a bit. I'm in no hurry. So long as you know what I feel then I'm happy.'

'It will be no use, Geoffrey.' She shook her head emphatically. 'I shall never fall in love with you so don't look for it to happen. You're doomed to disappointment if you hope I'll mellow or relent. I'm sorry this had to come up between us. I'm sure it will spoil our friendship.'

'I haven't been feeling friendly towards you for a very long time now.' His face was suddenly bleak and finely drawn, and his tones wavered slightly. 'I love you, Diana, more than anything else in this world; I love you. I've been aching to tell you for a very long time. You can't be serious when you say you have no feelings for me. I sense that you were made for me.'

He turned to her fiercely, carried away by his emotions, and Diana gasped in surprise when he seized hold of her and thrust her back upon the warm sand. The next instant he was hovering over her, raining kisses upon her face and neck. For a moment she was too surprised to resist, and then she exerted her strength and tried to push him off.

'Diana, I'm crazy about you,' he panted as he raised himself slightly. He looked into her eyes, and she caught her breath at sight of the emotion filling him. 'I love you to distraction. The thoughts of you are beginning to affect my work. What can I do but tell you I love you? If you turn me down my life will become meaningless. I shall have nothing to live for.'

'Let me go, Geoffrey, and try to control yourself,' she said. She realized that her tones were harsh and unrelenting, and the very touch of his mouth against hers made her feel unclean after the great pleasure she had derived from Fenton Leigh's kisses. 'I'm sorry,' she said in gentler tones. 'Please let me get up, Geoffrey. You took me by surprise! I had no idea you felt like this.'

'Then you'll consider what I've said?' he

demanded eagerly, getting to his feet and pulling her upright.

'I'm afraid you have nothing to hope for!' She shook her head and sighed. 'I don't wish to hurt you, but I have no feelings at all. It would be wrong for me to pretend that I had.'

His face showed his disappointment, and for a moment he was motionless, suspended in agony as he accepted her words. Then he shook his head slowly and sighed heavily.

'I'm sorry, Geoffrey,' she said again, and he nodded slowly and turned away. She walked behind him as he started off the beach. Her sympathies were aroused, and she reached out and touched his arm. 'Geoffrey, I'm so sorry.'

'Leave me. You've told me how we stand, so leave it at that.'

She halted in her tracks and he continued, and she did not move until he had disappeared among the trees. Then a bitter sigh escaped her and her shoulders slumped. She had slipped from her high pinnacle of emotion, brought down to earth by his unexpected declaration of love. She returned to the water's edge and walked along the fringe of white sand, wanting to outrun her thoughts, hoping to lose the sharpness of her feelings in physical activity. But now she was confused, and thoughts of the passion Fenton Leigh had aroused in her clashed with her pity for Geoffrey.

Why couldn't she fall in love with a steady man like Geoffrey? The question trembled through her. Why did a mysterious man have so much power over her mind? These feelings that were growing up inside her, were they the beginnings of love, or had passion laid its red-hot fingers upon her mind? She knew she couldn't tell the difference between one emotion or the other, and that further confused her. She was unsettled as she started out along the rocky promontory that ended in a jumble of obdurate rock crouching in eternal defiance of the waves. Spray flew high through the air when the wind was strong, and the promontory seemed to shudder and tremble when the storm waves came pounding in. But this evening was gentle, and the water was in caressing mood. Diana reached the tip of the finger and sat down on her favourite stone. She stared speculatively into the glittering sea.

What had come upon her? Was it a form of madness? Surely a man alone could not arouse so many deep and beguiling passions in a woman's breast. Had he placed some kind of a spell upon her? For a moment she was frightened. She knew all about the black magic which was supposed to exist in the islands. But white people were supposed to be above its reach, if they did not dabble in it, and Diana, as a doctor, had more reason than most to doubt its sinister power. But something had happened to her attitude of mind. Her peacefulness was gone and her head was filled with nagging thought. Fenton Leigh was responsible for that, and Diana came slowly to the decision that nothing would alter until she saw him again!

She stood up violently, vowing never to see Fenton again! He wouldn't rule her life! She had so many important things to do. Too many people relied on her! She was not free to act in a thoughtless or carefree manner. She was tied to her duty, like a soldier or a policeman, and if she didn't hold the same devotion to her duty then she was not fit to be what she was!

Her blue eyes flickered to the horizon, and her heart seemed to miss a few beats when she spotted a sail in the middle distance, then picked out the shape of a schooner. Her eyes widened, and she strained to make out details. The ship was coming towards St Flavia! It could only be Fenton's craft. She had never seen another like it in these waters!

All her intentions collapsed before the

excitement she felt. Her breathing seemed ragged, catching in her constricted throat, and when she imagined being held in Fenton's arms again she was swamped by a surfeit of unusual feelings.

Minutes passed and she didn't take her eyes from the ship. It was certainly heading for the cove where she waited, and it would be like Fenton, she guessed, to drop anchor at the point on the coast nearest to her father's plantation. The knowledge that he might be coming especially to see her made her think of other things, and she wondered if she were tidy enough for him.

The schooner came on swiftly, making for the shore, and soon Diana could make out the small figures on its deck. But she could not recognize Fenton, and disappointment began to fill her. She wanted now more than ever to see him, and her heart ached for a glimpse of him. Then she saw the Polynesian standing in the bows and her relief was tremendous. This was the *Argo!* Fenton had come for her!

When she saw him standing on the deck her emotions threatened to overwhelm her. She was trembling with suppressed excitement, and could hardly believe that this was really herself. She had never felt like this before, and her cheeks flamed as she realized that in

Fenton's company she was without shame.

When he spotted her he waved, and Diana waved instantly, filled with soaring hope. He had come to see her! He had waited for her to return to him, but when she hadn't arrived he had come to her! She tried to still the fast beating of her heart. She clenched her hands as her feelings became too much for her to contain. She longed to feel the strength of his arms about her, and she wanted more than anything to feel his mouth against hers, giving and demanding satisfaction.

The anchor splashed into the sea and the ship rode serenely. The dinghy came off the deck and Fenton's tall muscular figure dropped into it. Diana watched in a foment of impatience, and she began to thrill as he rowed towards the shore. There was a lump in her throat that no amount of swallowing could remove, and she could do nothing about the fluttering sensation in her breast. Now she didn't stop to think of the rights and wrongs of this affair. All she wanted was his embrace.

She could see the wolfish smile upon his darkly handsome face before he reached the rocks, and she waved again, her reserve gone, her eagerness apparent. Within a few moments he was at the spot where she stood, leaping out of the boat and dropping a small anchor into a crevice. Then he turned to her, standing erect and strong, his brown eyes smouldering with carefully controlled emotion.

'Well! This is a surprise! I came to find you and discover you waiting on the shore for me. How did you know I was coming?'

'I didn't! I wasn't waiting for you! I usually relax after a long day by walking the shore. When I spotted your ship I didn't know it was you at first.'

'But you're pleased to see me! I can tell by your face. And you're even more beautiful than the impression my mind retained. I waited for you to return to St Lydia, but you didn't come.'

'My time is limited, and after duty I have no way of travelling across the distance.'

'So I've come to you. I have all the time in the world!' He moved towards her, then held her in his arms, and Diana caught her breath, standing motionless for what seemed an eternal second, suspended in animation while she collected the vivid impressions of the moment for future reference. The soft murmur of the sea filled her ears with magic that soothed away doubt, the invitation of his arms drawing her as surely as metal is attracted to a magnet.

Diana uttered a little cry and pushed herself forward, throwing herself into his arms with wanton abandon. Her mind blanked out under the flooding emotions their embrace released inside her, and she felt like a tired swimmer in a choppy sea as he kissed her and pounded her with his magnetism and power.

'Diana, I thought you had forgotten me, or had second thoughts about me,' he whispered in her ear. 'Why didn't you come to me?'

'I couldn't. I have a job to do and I just can't turn my back on it,' she protested.

'But you wanted to come, didn't you?' His tones were gentle, compelling, and Diana nodded eagerly.

'I did, although I don't pretend to understand what you've done to me!' Her blue eyes were wide and appealing, and he laughed in his throat and kissed her again, powerfully, drawing every ounce of emotion from her mind. She sagged against him, physically drained by his strength and domination. She closed her eyes and let herself drift away from reality. Nothing seemed to matter now! She was finding peace for the first time since leaving his arms on St Lydia!

When he moved away from her she sank down upon a rock and stared into his face. He sat down opposite, his big figure at home in the rough setting. His face was composed, his eyes alive with bright emotion. He smiled, his even teeth glinting in the fine evening. His hands, large and powerful, yet gentle when they touched her, were clasped before him, his long, supple fingers interlaced in repose.

'So you feel the same things I do!' He nodded slowly. 'I told you there was something between us. We're strangers, and yet we're not. You're a highly respectable woman, but you threw yourself into my arms when I arrived, and this is only our third meeting. What's in your mind, Diana?'

'I couldn't begin to tell you,' she replied breathlessly. 'I don't know myself, and I won't pretend to know what's happening. I fear you have placed some spell upon me. I am quite helpless in your presence, and completely unhappy away from you.'

'This is the way I feel!' His eyes seemed to glow as he studied her face. 'So what do you think is happening to us?'

'I daren't think.' She shuddered as emotion started working inside her again. 'I don't think you're serious about me. You know the effect you have on me, and you're exploiting it for your own amusement.'

'No. Don't ever think that. Let your heart be your guide, Diana.'

She looked into his face, saw the steadiness

in his brown eyes, and let her eyes follow the lean line of his jaw. His mouth was composed, his lips full and generous, and she felt a pang stab through her as she tried to fight down her raging desire.

'I must let my head rule me,' she said unsteadily. 'I must be strong against you and forbid myself ever to see you again.'

'Why?'

'Because I am a doctor and have my duty to do. I can't let myself be overwhelmed by emotion! You're a stranger to me, Fenton, and I feel certain that you're just playing some kind of a cruel game with me. Why? What is it you intend doing to me?'

'You tell me!' He shook his head slowly. 'I suppose you have been listening to all the scandal about me since we parted on St Lydia!' His eyes narrowed and a tight smile touched his lips. 'It would be only natural for you to want to learn all you can about my past. I don't blame you, Diana.'

'I haven't once heard your name mentioned since that day I left you,' she retorted. 'And what is there for me to learn that I don't already know?'

'I leave that to you to find out. I have done nothing of which to be ashamed, you may rest assured, but people being what they are, as soon as scandal attached itself to my name

I was accused of every other crime in the book. But that has nothing to do with us, here and now, Diana. I'm in love with you and I want to continue seeing you at every opportunity. But there's the rub. You are the doctor, and as such you have a certain degree of respectability to maintain. Your patients, the whites I mean, would be shocked to know that your healing hands have touched me, that I have thrilled you with kisses as you've never been thrilled before. I think you're going to find yourself in deep water before very long, and as soon as people discover that you're seeing me.'

'I don't care what people think!'

'At the moment you don't because you've never had the weight of public opinion against you. But the people in these islands are very narrow-minded, and I know that better than anyone. You had better think carefully about your future, Diana.'

'My future is mapped out for me, and has been so for a good many years,' she retorted, trying to maintain her control. But her tones were wavering under the pressure, and she was trembling deep inside.

'That's what you think. Where do I fit in?' His voice was insistent, and Diana longed to throw herself into his arms. 'Well?' he went on when she made no reply.

She was thinking of the uneasiness which had gripped her in the days following their parting on St Lydia. She had wanted him so very badly! Even her duty had seemed to lose its importance in the face of her burning emotions. When she had seen his ship approaching this evening she had felt very much like a castaway sighting a rescue ship after many long years of solitude and frustration. But there was a speck of sanity in her mind, planted there by her years of studying and training, and she knew deep inside that she couldn't throw everything away for the sake of this strangely compelling man. She had to call a halt now. If she were to have any chance of success then she had to terminate this wonderful affair before it was too late, before the last of her determination fled.

'I'm afraid this must be the last time we see each other, Fenton, because nothing good will come of it. You're already beginning to dominate me, and I must be free to do my duty. You're the most disconcerting man I've ever met, and I shall be torn between my desires and my need to do my duty. I can't face such a prospect, so you'd better go and forget about me.'

'Better you should ask me to forget that I'm alive!' He got to his feet and towered over her.

She looked up at him, her eyes filled with sadness. 'It's too late now to try and forget you. I've been searching for you too long to give up now that I've found you. There's no one else. You told me that! There's no earthly reason why we shouldn't get together as God intended!'

'No. I lied to you.' Desperation filled Diana. She knew this was her only chance of staying clear of him. Love could only come second in her life! Duty was a harsh mistress, and ruled with inflexible will. 'There is a man in my life, and this very evening he said he wanted to marry me.'

Fenton stared at her with shock showing in his face and eyes, and Diana felt stricken by the pain which must now be flooding him. But her reason told her that she had to make a stand now or go under in the struggle that would surely follow. She was not a normal woman with an ordinary life to lead. She had placed herself in the service of the community, and she could not go back on her oath now. She could not become one man's slave, although that life promised Heaven through the years. She had to turn her back upon him and keep him out of sight and out of mind. It was the only way, and she accepted it against all her womanly desires.

'I'm sorry, Fenton! But you must go, and never try to see me again.'

He stared into her face, trying to discount her words, but she kept her face expressionless and her eyes blank, and the silence that closed in about them seemed to sign her decision. Then he turned without a word and set his boat adrift, leaping into it and rowing away quickly. He didn't look at her as the distance between them increased, and Diana turned and hurried away before he reached the ship!

CHAPTER FIVE

Diana could understand some of the misery that Geoffrey Foster must be feeling because of her denial of him. She felt as if her heart was being torn asunder as she hurried home, and she had to fight the desire to turn and run back to the shore, to summon Fenton back and tell him that she wanted him. The fact that they were still strangers didn't seem to have any effect on her. Time was as nothing when two people met and discovered that they were soul-mates, fashioned for one another in that ecstatic world all lovers dream about. She knew in her heart that he was special, that he could have become the greatest thing in her entire life, but she had the sense to see that he would clash with her way of life, and she was not prepared to give up medicine. She could not give it up! She was not free to do so! Medicine held her in an inexorable grip and would never relent. She knew this, and was determined that nothing would be given the chance to drive a wedge through her life.

When she reached home she found a restlessness inside her that was hard to control. She felt sick at heart, utterly depressed, and there seemed no way of alleviating the situation. She saw Geoffrey seated on the verandah of his bungalow, and wanted to go to him, wanted to tell him what had happened to her, to inform him that she knew some of the misery he was experiencing. But she kept out of sight and prayed that her mind would accept the bitter facts and give her some peace later.

It was a strain trying to appear normal in front of her parents, when she wanted to break down and cry for the love she had deserted. She still couldn't fully understand how a stranger could enter her heart and do so much irreparable damage. She had always thought herself immune to love and that sort of thing. Romance had been something of a mystery in which other normal people indulged, and that was all she had cared about it. But now she knew better about it!

Sitting with her mother later that evening, Diana tried to maintain her usual light-hearted chatter, but she was beginning to feel the effects of her depression, and impatience flared inside her. Mrs Brett, sensing that something had taken place recently which might lead to great changes in the family, began asking questions destined to give Diana the opportunity of talking about love and Geoffrey, and Diana's heart ached as she tried to find the right words to say to her mother. But before they could get down to cases Vinia Owen appeared at the door with the information that Mrs Reid was calling.

'Show her in, Vinia,' Lillian Brett said eagerly. She half turned to Diana. 'She did ring earlier and said that she might be calling. She's hot on the news about the Leighs.'

'What news is that?' Diana demanded, interested despite her strict rule never to indulge in gossip. 'I haven't heard anything.'

'You're never interested enough to want to learn anything,' her mother reproved. 'But if you want to know, there is talk that the Leigh plantation is to be sold. Your father is interested in it. He would like to take over on St Lydia, and in all probability we would move to the other island to live.'

'This is all news to me!' Diana stiffened in her seat, and her mind worked fast as a mill race as she tried to see the significance in what her mother had said.

At that moment Vinia reappeared, followed closely by Mrs Reid. Diana studied their neighbour's fleshy, wrinkled face. Alice Reid was a widow of about fifty-seven, and had a manager to run her late husband's plantation. She spent most of her time visiting people on the island, for she had a morbid curiosity in the business of her neighbours. She was certain to be the first to learn of any secret changes, almost before they had been planned, and she was the focal point for gossip. She smiled now at Diana as she paused on the threshold of the room, and for a heart-stopping moment Diana couldn't help wondering if the woman had learned something of her involvement with Fenton Leigh.

'Alice, it's so nice of you to drop in again. I thought you were visiting the Rutherford place this evening.'

'Eileen Rutherford telephoned to say they couldn't manage it this evening. They're having trouble with their daughter Jane, and she's gone missing, of all things.'

'Missing?' Lillian Brett glanced a little

sheepishly at Diana, well knowing her daughter's feelings about gossip but she wanted to learn the latest, and she fetched Alice Reid a drink and sat down at the woman's side. Diana listened intently, not so much for the gossip but to learn what was being said about the Leigh plantation.

'Jane has been acting strangely for some time,' Mrs Reid said in her scratchy, tale-telling voice. 'They've done everything to prevent a rebellion, but Jane has disappeared. I heard that she was seen talking to Fenton Leigh in Tenka early this afternoon. I don't know if she visited his ship with him, but she hasn't been seen since.'

Diana felt herself going cold, and her flesh crawled at the woman's words. She struggled to keep her face expressionless, and fought the urge to say what she thought about gossip-mongering.

'There are so many stories about Fenton Leigh that one doesn't know really what to believe,' Mrs Brett mused. 'Was the girl actually seen going aboard the ship, Alice?'

'Not actually, but you know what's happened in the past. He was never any different, was he? I seem to remember a lot of talk about him before he finished with medicine. Now he's back, and it hasn't taken him long to start his old tricks.' Mrs Reid turned suddenly to address Diana. 'Have you ever met him, Diana?'

'Yes, I have, as a matter of fact; the other afternoon in Tope.' Diana sighed a little as she replied. 'But what was I supposed to do, swoon into his arms?'

'A lot of women have,' Mrs Reid said cautiously. 'But then, you're not like the rest of us, are you? You're above that sort of thing. You have to be, being a doctor, although being a doctor didn't stop Fenton Leigh!'

Diana started to her feet, unable to listen to any more, but her mother began asking questions about the Leigh plantation, and Diana changed her original intention from stalking from the room to crossing to the window and staring out across the yard. She listened to the chatter going on at her back, and her face reddened as she considered what had already been said. Had Fenton got that girl aboard his ship? Had she been there even while he had come ashore to see her? Diana felt moved to anger, but it was directed against herself and not Fenton.

'There is talk that Willard Leigh is ashamed that his brother has returned to the islands,' Mrs Reid was saying quickly. 'I don't blame him after what happened, and I suppose it is only natural to hate Fenton. All men hate him!

I can remember my husband talking about Fenton just the year before he died. He said even I wouldn't have been safe with Fenton around. But he was completely disinherited at one time, and it was a great surprise to all of us when the will was read and it was discovered that Fenton still had half the estate.'

'I don't think he's as black as he's painted,' Mrs Brett said. 'They always add a lot of things to a character like that.'

'So they do, but don't forget that several people died in mysterious circumstances while Fenton was a doctor. He was found guilty of unprofessional conduct and struck off the roll.'

'But he was not found guilty of actually killing a patient,' Diana felt constrained to say. 'They gave him the benefit of the doubt, remember.'

'It was done to save the reputation of all doctors,' Mrs Reid said firmly.

'If you think that then you'll believe anything, and from what you tell my mother from time to time I'm inclined to think that she's as bad as you are.' Diana turned to face them, her eyes flaring with anger. 'Perhaps there is some excuse for you, Mrs Reid, living alone as you do, but my mother ought to know better than to indulge in this sort of thing.'

'Diana!' Mrs Brett got quickly to her feet.

'How can you say such a thing?'

'It's perfectly true, Mother!' Diana had no intention of backing down, and she was further angry with herself for wanting to stick up for Fenton.

'I notice you listened eagerly enough when Fenton's name was first mentioned,' Mrs Reid said affably. She was not in the least put out by Diana's outburst, and she smiled maddeningly. 'Perhaps you found him more to your liking than you care to admit! But you're not the only one! No woman is safe where he is concerned. Even I would think twice before permitting myself to be alone with him.'

Diana sighed and turned on her heel, leaving the room, and she went out into the yard, feeling hot and angry. Before she realized it she had crossed to Geoffrey's bungalow, and she paused when he got to his feet, the expression on his face warning her that she had acted thoughtlessly.

'Geoffrey, I'm sorry to burst in on you like this,' she said lamely.

'That's all right. Feel free to come over any time you like.' He watched her with eyes that might have belonged to a sick dog. 'I wanted to see you, anyway. I'd like to apologize for what happened down on the shore earlier.'

'Apologize? For telling a woman that you

love her?' She shook her head. 'There's nothing to apologize for, Geoff. You paid me a compliment, and I'm truly sorry that I couldn't return it.'

'I know. We won't go into that any more. I'm going to try and forget it.'

'We're still friends?' she asked.

'Forever.' He nodded emphatically. 'I feel relieved now that I've seen you again. I thought you would cut me dead after this.'

'Nonsense! You've done nothing to be ashamed of.'

'Like a drink?' He relaxed visibly. 'Please sit down. Let's talk for a bit, shall we?'

Diana accepted a drink, and she sat down, but she was in no mood for chatting, and after several minutes she finished the drink and got to her feet. She felt that she would never be able to sit still again! The pain in her breast was getting worse all the time. Deep inside there was an urge that tried to make her forget everything and go seek Fenton out. She was praying that it would settle, that she could master it and stamp it out, but there would be a long period of agony before the matter was finally settled.

'Geoff, I'm going back to the house,' she said suddenly, cutting across his words, and he got quickly to his feet.

'Have I said something wrong?' he

demanded in great fear.

'No!' She shook her head. 'I'm tired and overwrought this evening. I'm not very good company. I think I'll go and turn in. I have rather a heavy day before me tomorrow, and I'd better get some rest.'

'I'll walk you across the yard.'

'Don't bother! Thanks for everything.' She hurried away and almost started running, and as she neared the house she was certain that she would not be able to stop, that her heart would overrule her mind and send her over the ridge and down to the shore in the vain hope that Fenton would still be waiting for her.

She clenched her hands as she reached the house, and when she entered she stood by the door of the lounge and listened to Mrs Reid's voice talking unending gossip. She took a long shuddering breath. This she couldn't take. Her mind was beginning to protest at the strain being imposed upon it. She had to do something to relieve the tension or she would never sleep through the night.

Vinia came through from the kitchen, and Diana was startled by the native woman's silent approach. Vinia smiled as Diana turned to her. She cocked her head and listened to the voices in the room, and she nodded vigorously.

'I don't blame you, Doctor Diana,' she said in a harsh whisper. 'That sort of thing isn't fit for your delicate ears.'

'I'm going back down to the shore for a swim, Vinia,' Diana said. 'Would you fetch my swimsuit and a towel, please?' She considered as the housekeeper started away obediently. 'I'll wait for you in the kitchen, Vinia. I want to slip out the back way so nobody sees where I'm going.'

'I understand.' Vinia laughed good-naturedly and went up the stairs.

Diana breathed steadily as she went into the kitchen. Already she was feeling easier! Just the decision to go back to the shore had settled her! She knew then that she was in for a bad time. Fenton Leigh was firmly embedded in her mind and she would find it no simple matter to get rid of him.

When she had her swimsuit and a towel, Diana left the house by the back door, informing Vinia to tell her mother where she was going only if Mrs Brett enquired after her. Hurrying into the trees that grew quite close to the rear of the house, Diana walked so fast along the path over the ridge that she was breathless by the time she reached the top. But it wasn't her exertions alone that caused her pulses to race and her heart to pound madly. She paused on the crest and her blue eyes swept the sea before her. When she saw the schooner still anchored in the cove her joy knew no bounds! He hadn't sailed away! He was probably waiting for her to return to the shore, and no doubt he was keeping a close watch upon the beach for any sign of life.

Diana found it difficult to breathe. She had no idea what lay beyond the strange power he seemed to exert, but she was aware that she was helpless in his hands, and right now she wanted nothing more than to feel his arms about her and his mouth against hers.

She hurried down to the beach, her pride gone, her thoughts only upon the pleasures she would find in his company. Evening was closing in, and already the horizon was indistinct. But Diana had swum in the night before, and she relished the thought of sneaking out to the schooner and surprising Fenton. She knew he must have been telling the truth or he wouldn't have remained. He knew she was trying to break free and he had been certain that she would find it impossible. Now she knew she couldn't win, and she would rather take what was coming in the way of scandal than suffer the agonies of being without him.

She changed into her swimsuit and left her clothes on the beach. Her body gleamed palely as night closed in swiftly, and already there were lights aboard the schooner, seeming to beckon her. She was ready to answer their call! Overhead, the deepening sky was suddenly clustered with countless chips of twinkling ice as the stars showed, and Diana entered the water and plunged down into the cool depths, holding her breath as she struck out furiously in an attempt to tire herself sufficiently to find sleep during the coming night.

There was a slight swell as she swam steadily towards the lights of the schooner, but the distance was no more than two hundred yards, and she was a powerful swimmer. In no time she was treading water in the bulk of the ship's shadow, and now she could not bring herself to announce her presence. What kind of a fool was she? What sort of trouble was she calling down upon her head? Sanity returned to her for a moment and she knew the futility of what she was doing. But the next instant she was feeling the burning of her desires and could not resist them. It didn't matter to her what he might think. She was madly in love with him, a fiery, passionate love that could not be quenched by her own efforts. It might burn itself out in a week under the pressures of his company, but it would never quench itself!

Diana trod water, her arms gleaming as

they moved in the dark water. She could hear the sound of voices aboard the craft, and there was music, muted by closed doors. The swell slapped gently at the hull of the ship, and Diana suddenly longed for the security of the big cabin aboard, where Fenton spent most of his time.

The next instant her attention was taken from the ship by a slight disturbance in the water at her side, and she gasped as something touched her in passing. Such was her shock that she inadvertently opened her mouth and swallowed a quantity of water. She went under, and was aware that some mysterious creature swam around her in the darkness. Fear for the unknown filled her and she almost panicked. But she kicked her way back to the surface and clawed for the side of the ship.

The dinghy was moored alongside the ship, and Diana hadn't noticed it before. Now she grabbed the side of it and lunged upwards, out of the water, striking her side and then her knees upon the rough wood. She fell in a heap into the dinghy, raising a clatter and barking her elbows painfully, but she was relieved to get out of the water away from that unknown creature.

The next instant the dinghy tipped alarmingly, and a dark figure loomed up out of the water, scrambling into the boat beside her, and she leaped to her feet and sprang for the side of the ship, a scream ringing out from her lips and echoing away across the dark water. She landed heavily upon the deck of the schooner, aware that the figure in the boat was leaping up behind her, and as she gave way to unreasoning panic she screamed again.

The deck was dark and she slithered across it, making for the companionway which led to Fenton's cabin, and behind her there was a sinister pattering sound upon the heavy wooden surface. She tried to scream again, but fear had constricted her throat. Then she saw light streaming out as the hatch over the companionway was suddenly thrown open. The light blinded her and she ran into some obdurate object that loomed up suddenly. As she struck it heavily she realized it was another dinghy, resting upon its supports on the deck, and their contact proved to be a stunning one. Diana's head struck the side of the dinghy and she lost consciousness quickly, hardly aware of the pain, but certainly aware that the creature which had followed her out of the sea was now gaining upon her in the shadows. She slumped to the deck and knew no more . . .

Coming back to consciousness was like rearing up out of the sea, but there was pain in Diana's head, and when she opened her eyes the light was too bright for her. She could hear a confused babble of voices, and wondered if she were taking part in some weird nightmare. Then she remembered the creature in the sea, and she opened her eyes again, fear closing in upon her.

The first thing she saw was Fenton's dark face peering anxiously at her, and she sighed her relief when she saw she was lying on the bunk in his cabin. Then at his shoulder appeared the face of the Polynesian, dripping wet and carrying a scared expression. In that instant realization came to her, and Fenton laughed shortly when he saw her changing expressions.

'So Zero frightened you, did he?' he demanded. 'Well I'm not surprised. He's pulled that trick on me once or twice when I've been swimming after dark. But he meant you no harm, and he's as worried about you as I am. He saw you in the water before you reached the side of the ship, and slipped in to check you out. He's better than a watchdog! But how are you feeling? You've lost some skin from various parts of you, and there's a whopping great bruise on your forehead where you tried to argue with the deck dinghy. As far as I can tell there are no bones broken, but the way you chose to come aboard isn't to be recommended.'

Diana took a deep breath, then sighed heavily. Her panic subsided, and she could see real concern in the Polynesian's dusky face. She slowly moved her arms and legs, and then sat up, gingerly feeling herself to ensure that no worse damage had befallen her. She found her elbows and knees skinned, and there was blood showing on her left knee. Her head ached, and when she lifted an exploring hand she found a large bump in the centre of her forehead.

'I seem to be all right,' she said unsteadily, and looked around the cabin, almost expecting to see the missing Jane Rutherford being held prisoner. But the cabin was otherwise empty, and it didn't look as if it had been used as a prison.

The Polynesian spoke rapidly in his own tongue and Fenton replied in similar manner. Then Fenton grinned.

'Zero wants to know if you're all right. Are you angry with him for scaring you?'

'Tell him no.' Diana winced as she shook her head. 'I'm all right, and he was only doing his job, I suppose.'

Fenton spoke to the native, who showed his teeth in a wide grin and turned to depart. Diana leaned back and closed her eyes for a moment.

'Do you mind if I rest for a few minutes?' she demanded in faint tones.

'Take as long as you like. You've had quite a shock.' His voice was gentle, slightly reproving. 'You gave me quite a shock, too. I never expected to see you again.'

Diana opened her eyes quickly and stared up at him, aware that his dark eyes were watching her. She suddenly felt very defenceless, stretched out upon his bunk and clad only in a two-piece swimsuit, but her head was aching too much for her to really care.

'I didn't swim out here to come aboard,' she said firmly, lifting a hand to press it against her head.

'Of course not,' he said soothingly.

'I was taking my customary swim, and perhaps I did come a bit too close to your ship, but I only came aboard because your man scared me out of the water.'

'I don't care about your excuses,' Fenton said mildly. 'I am the first one to admit that this cove is public, and one can swim wherever one pleases. But you have come aboard my ship, and I've been thinking quite deeply about you. For a moment I had wild hopes that you had had second thoughts about what you said on the shore earlier. But I can see by your manner that you haven't relented, and I'm sorry. I didn't sail away immediately I returned, because I wanted to give you time to think it over. But if you are still certain that there can be nothing in the future for the both of us then I'll sail away and never come back. I intend returning to my old haunts in the Pacific.'

'No!' The word came straight from Diana's heart. She opened her eyes and stared up at him. 'I can't go on pretending, Fenton,' she said slowly, deliberately. 'Of course I swam out here again this evening to see you. I can't get you out of my thoughts. I don't want to live without you. I can't pretend to understand any of this, but I do know that you're the only man I shall ever want, and if I can't have you I might as well be dead.'

Her voice echoed for a moment, and then she relaxed and lay watching him. Fenton stared down at her, his face immobile, set in expressionless lines that gave away none of his thoughts. Then he nodded slowly, as if coming to a decision.'

'I was hoping you would come to this,' he said huskily. 'I know I'm right in saying that we do have a good future together. All I ask is that I get the chance to prove it.'

'You'll get the chance,' Diana told him. 'With all my heart, you'll get the chance!'

CHAPTER SIX

It was quite late when Fenton rowed Diana back to the beach, and they stood for a moment at the spot where she had left her clothes. The tropical night was so peaceful, and the moon was very full and low in the sky, hanging silently over the silvered sea, and even the tiny wavelets lapping the beach seemed to have magic in their sound. Diana was exalted. She had never felt so high before. She had never imagined, even in her wildest dreams, that a man could make a woman so happy. She overlooked the fact that they were still almost complete strangers. He excited and thrilled her beyond all comprehension, and that was sufficient.

'When am I going to see you again, Diana?' he whispered in her ear. His powerful figure was shapeless before her, in the dense shadows under the trees, and Diana wriggled her bare toes in the sand as she looked into his darkened face. She could see his eyes glinting, and his teeth showed when he spoke. She could not prevent a heavy sigh escaping her. 'You're not going to change your mind again, are you?' he demanded.

'No!' She shook her head, her hands pressed against his broad shoulders. 'I could never find the strength to stay away from you, Fenton. But I don't know when I'll be able to see you again. My days are so busy! I travel around the islands! How will I know where to find you?'

'I'll be living on my ship in the cove here for a few days,' he replied. 'Come and see me whenever you're off duty.' He paused and kissed her. 'Perhaps you'll want to keep all this secret for a spell,' he went on. 'Knowing how people talk about me, you may not want your name publicly linked with mine. You are a doctor, and should be above reproach, you know.'

'I don't care about what people think,' she retorted passionately. 'I love you and you love me! What does it matter about your past? As I see it, you've done no wrong!'

'I wish they would all think like that!' His tones were low, filled with resignation. 'But I don't care about myself, Diana. It's you I'm worried about. Medicine is your whole life. It was mine once, but I had to give it up, and I can clearly remember the agonies I suffered at the time. Any love you feel for me would be cancelled out by such trouble. Then you would have nothing.'

'I'll take my chances as I see them. I know

how I feel, Fenton.'

A rustling sound in the shadows behind them made Diana start nervously, so wrapped up had she been in the man she loved. Fenton moved quickly and half stepped around her, ready to protect her if necessary, and Diana froze a little inside when she saw a figure materializing slowly from the surrounding darkness. Her breath caught in her throat as a straying beam of moonlight touched the face of the newcomer and she saw it was Geoffrey Foster. Relief, mingled with worry, laced through her, and she discovered she was holding her breath, and it escaped her slowly.

'Diana! Where the devil have you been?' Foster demanded. He craned forward to look at her, and a gasp escaped him. 'What on earth are you doing dressed like that at this time of the night?' He peered at Fenton, and gasped again when he recognized him. 'Fenton Leigh! Diana, are you out of your mind?'

'What do you mean by that, Geoff?' Diana was instantly aroused.

'Well look at you! In a swimsuit at midnight, and in his company!' There was no mistaking the tone of Foster's voice, and the knowledge that everyone looked down upon the man she loved stung Diana.

'What do you read into the situation,

Geoff?' she demanded in dangerously steady tones. 'Tell me and then I'll tell you what happened.'

Foster made no reply, and Diana gulped at the lump in her throat, knowing that she dared not tell the truth. She would have to lie if an explanation were to be made. The knowledge hurt her even more. She wanted to be proud of her feelings!

'I was swimming out by the ship,' she said dully. 'I got into difficulties and Mr Leigh took me aboard.'

'You went swimming earlier! Have you just come ashore?' There was sharp suspicion in Foster's tones.

'I don't think I like your tone,' Fenton said thinly. 'What business is it of yours, anyway?'

'I'm making it my business, where you're concerned.'

'I don't think we've ever met. What do you know about me?'

'I don't have to know you to know about you!' Geoffrey came forward an angry pace, and Diana caught her breath as she realized that they would soon be squaring up to one another. She pushed herself between them.

'Please stop this!' Her voice was tight with suppressed emotion. 'Geoffrey, I don't need your services as a nurse. I am well able to take care of myself, and I want you to know that Mr Leigh has been a perfect gentleman.'

'What happened to Jane Rutherford, Leigh?' Geoffrey demanded angrily.

'Jane Rutherford?' Fenton shook his head. 'I don't know what you mean. Who is Jane Rutherford?'

'You were talking to her on the quayside at Tenka early this afternoon, and now she's gone missing. Is she aboard that ship of yours?'

'Geoffrey!' Diana could not keep the anger out of her tones. 'What on earth will you be saying next? You'd better go now, before this situation gets out of hand.'

Fenton stood tall and immobile in the shadows, and she could not see his expression. But Diana guessed he was angry. She clenched her hands and tried to control her own temper.

'So this is the reason why you wouldn't admit that you are in love with me,' Geoffrey said tersely. 'You've met this man! Until a few days ago I was certain that you loved me. Everything pointed to it, Diana! But now he's come along and charmed every shred of decency out of you.'

Diana gasped again, and lifted her hand to slap Geoffrey hard. But Fenton moved forward, and the next instant there was the sharp sound of a blow. Geoffrey cried out in shock and sudden pain and crumpled to the sand. Fenton stood over him, and when he spoke his voice was trembling with anger.

'You'll apologize for that,' he commanded. 'Get up and tell Diana that you're sorry you ever had the thought.'

'Please!' Diana pulled at Fenton's shoulder, but she might try to push one of the beach palms aside for all the effect she had upon him. 'Let him up, Fenton. Violence isn't the answer.'

'He insulted you and he's going to say sorry!' Fenton said doggedly. 'Usually it's the women who gossip about me, and I can't strike back. But when a man's guilty of saying things like this then there's cause for me to get upset.'

Geoffrey scrambled to his feet and faced them. He seemed a slim youth in contrast to Fenton's powerful bulk, but he lifted his fists and came forward. Diana cried out and thrust herself between them.

'Stop this nonsense!' she commanded. 'Geoffrey, mind your own business and leave here immediately. You have no right to interfere with my life, and as for your remarks about my feelings towards you, I told you earlier exactly how I feel about you, and I shall never change my mind.'

The two men stood facing one another in

silence, and Diana knew they didn't hear her harsh words. They were acting out an age-old instinct and nothing could prevent trouble. But Fenton suddenly relaxed and stepped back. He stared down into Diana's face.

'I've seen you safely back on shore,' he said politely. 'Now I must return to my ship. Goodbye, Diana.'

'Goodbye, Mr Leigh, and thank you for this evening.' She wanted to throw herself into his arms and be kissed by him, to proclaim her love to anyone who would care to listen, but she knew she was tightly bound by convention and so she acted a part that she hated because she was afraid of what people might say about her, despite her protestations to the contrary when Fenton told her she would act like this.

Fenton grinned briefly and turned away, and Diana remained motionless until she heard the scrape of the dinghy on the sand then the splash as the little boat met the water. The next moment her ears detected the sound of oars, and she relaxed a little and let her breath escape her in a long, shuddering sigh.

'And now, if you'll depart, Geoffrey,' she said in freezing tones, 'I'll get dressed.'

'I'll wait for you along the path,' he said thinly.

'No need for that. I know my way around, and I'm not afraid of the dark.'

'I want to talk to you!'

'There's nothing you can say will make any difference to what I feel, and I'm equally certain that you'll never be able to repair the breach you've made in our friendship. Now will you please go? I want to get dressed.'

He stood his ground, one hand to his face where Fenton's fist had struck him, and Diana stared at him for a moment, then sighed heavily and bent to pick up her clothes. She pulled on her skirt over her swimsuit, which was dry, anyway, and slipped into her blouse with impatient, angry movements. Geoffrey stood motionless until she was ready to leave the beach, and when she strode off through the trees without a word to him he followed silently.

Diana maintained a fast pace over the ridge and down the reverse slope, and she was breathless by the time she reached the yard. She studied the darkened house for a moment, but did not glance behind. She knew Geoffrey was there because she could hear his breathlessness, but she didn't want to talk to him, and started towards the house with determination in every fibre of her body.

'Diana! Wait!' His voice was filled with agony. 'Please listen to me! I lost my head back there because I love you so very much. I didn't mean the half of what I said. It was just the shock of seeing you with that man!'

'Keep your voice down!' She turned to him. 'Do you want to awaken my parents? What's got into you, Geoffrey? You've never acted like this before! You're not my keeper, you know!'

'I'm well aware of that. But until this evening I was nursing a secret. You know that secret now, and I feel responsible for you. I want to watch out for you, to help you avoid any mistakes that might crop up.'

'Any temptations, don't you mean?' She was still angry. 'You had no right to talk like that, did you?'

'I know. But I saw red when I recognized him. Any respectable girl wouldn't want to be seen dead within a mile of him.'

'That's a dreadful thing to say and you know it. People talk about him, but I've found nothing wrong with him.'

'How long have you known him?' he countered.

'That's beside the point. From what you and all the others say a girl isn't safe from the first minute in his company. But I didn't find him a bit like that.' She caught her breath and half turned away. 'Now I'm going in to bed.

I'm tired and I have a busy day ahead of me tomorrow.'

'Goodnight!' He sounded contrite now. 'Let's talk about this tomorrow, when we'll both have subsided a little.'

'There's nothing to talk about,' she responded firmly, and walked on to the house. She didn't look back, but as she paused at the front door she heard the door of his bungalow close noisily. Some of her passion left her then, and she felt quite weak and she went in to bed . . .

Next morning she was awake early, filled with the need to do a great deal, and she checked her schedules and found that she was due to fly to Tuna and St Lydia. She decided to go to Tuna first, and sought out Jerry Todd. The little pilot was waiting for her, and his weather-beaten face creased into a grin when he saw her approaching along the waterfront.

'Jerry, are you all set for the day?' she demanded, and her eyes glanced past the trim lines of the seaplane riding its moorings and spotted Fenton's schooner anchored several hundred yards out in the bay.

'I'm all ready. But you're just too late to see the fun.' Todd watched her face with intent blue eyes.

'What fun?' Instinctively, Diana knew he

was talking about Fenton, and fear closed in around her heart as she stared into the little pilot's face.

'The police arrested Fenton Leigh this morning!'

The words hit Diana like a hurricane, and she gasped aloud. Her face paled beneath its tan, and Jerry frowned as he saw her reactions.

'You all right, Doctor?' he demanded. 'You're not another of these females who can't resist Fenton Leigh, are you?'

'Don't be absurd, Jerry,' she retorted desperately. 'I don't know the man at all.'

'You spent some considerable time with him at St Lydia the other afternoon, and I've already heard that you were aboard his schooner last evening.'

'You've heard that!' Diana was jolted by the news. 'Where on earth did you get it from?'

'Inspector Pollard was asking questions when he brought Fenton ashore here, and I heard Leigh say that you were in his company last night. I expect the Inspector will want to see you.'

'But why has Fenton Leigh been arrested?' she demanded, unable to keep anxiety out of her tones.

'Haven't you heard that Jane Rutherford

has gone missing?'

'So?' Diana's tones were sharp.

'She was seen down here on the quayside yesterday afternoon, and afterwards she vanished. But while she was here she spoke to Fenton Leigh. He was ashore for a spell.'

'What does that prove?'

'Search me! But the Inspector must have some information implicating Leigh or he wouldn't have taken such a drastic step as arresting him.'

Diana stood rooted to the spot for a moment, unable to think clearly. But she could not believe that Fenton would have anything to do with a girl's disappearance. He wasn't as black as he was painted. No matter what he had done in the past, he had never willingly hurt anyone. He had been a doctor, and that proved he cared about other people. His reputation for being a devil where women were concerned might have been built up by jealous women.

'Well, do we leave right away?' Jerry demanded. 'We're all ready to go. It's Tuna first, isn't it?'

'Yes. Put my bag in the cockpit, will you, Jerry? Have you got the medical supplies aboard?'

'All taken care of,' he reported. 'One crate for the mission on Tuna and two for the clinic on St Lydia. But where are you going?'

'To the police station. If I can help clear up this mystery then it's my duty to do so. I won't be a few minutes.'

She was aware that Jerry eyed her intently as she turned away, and she hurried along the quay to the large white building that housed the police station. There was a native policeman on duty at the door, and he saluted as she approached. She entered the building, filled with determination, and enquired at the desk inside for Inspector Pollard. When she gave her name to the native sergeant he beamed at her and hurried into a nearby office. Within a few seconds Diana was being shown into the Inspector's office.

'Doctor Brett! It's very good of you to come along. I was planning to see you sometime today, although I know you are an extremely busy person.' Pollard was a tall, powerfully built man of weatherbeaten appearance, and his sharp features were accentuated by a beetling moustache that was greying slightly. He was an alert man with grey eyes that bespoke of his long experience in searching out the truth, and Diana knew him well. Her parents were prominent members of the social circle in which the Inspector moved. 'Are you here in connection with Fenton Leigh?' he asked.

'Yes, Inspector. I heard that he had been arrested!' There was tension in Diana's tones.

'Arrested! Good Lord no! I brought him in for questioning, and he's still helping my enquiries, but he certainly hasn't been arrested. I don't even know if a crime has been committed!'

'Oh!' Diana felt some flushing of relief through her veins, and her voice quivered. 'I heard that he had to account for his movements last night, and as I was aboard his ship for several hours I thought I'd better volunteer the information to save you a lot of needless questioning.'

'I see.' Inspector Pollard's pale eyes bored into Diana's as if they would break down her exterior and reveal all that lay in her mind. 'I'm not really so concerned about his movements last night, although I would like to know how he was occupied. You went aboard the schooner last evening, you say? What time was that, and at what time did you leave?'

Diana told him, keeping nothing back, and saw that her words were believed. She sighed heavily as she ended up with her report of what had happened on the beach between Fenton and Geoffrey. Pollard's face did not change expression when he learned of the violence that had flared.

'I'll be having a chat with Geoffrey Foster later,' he said. 'Now, while you were aboard the schooner did you see any sign of Jane Rutherford?'

'Not at all!'

'Did you hear a woman's voice, or see any item of clothing that would have indicated the presence of a woman?'

'Nothing at all.' Diana shook her head. She couldn't admit that she had really gone aboard in the first place to satisfy herself that the missing girl wasn't there. Now she was more certain than ever that Jane Rutherford hadn't gone aboard the schooner after talking to Fenton on the quay.

Pollard himself seemed more certain, and he got to his feet and showed Diana to the door. 'Thank you for coming in, Doctor,' he said. 'You've certainly proved that Leigh is telling the truth, although he didn't mention the trouble he had on the beach with Geoffrey Foster. I have no intention of arresting Leigh for anything. As I said, I don't know that a crime has been committed. But a girl is missing and it is my duty to check up on all the people who saw her just before she disappeared, to find out, if I can, what attitude she had or if she made any plans for taking a trip.'

'I'll be on my way then, Inspector. I have

to go to Tuna today, then on to St Lydia, so I shall be pretty busy. If you should want to talk to me again you'll have to wait until this evening.'

'That's all right, Doctor. I'll always be able to contact you, should I want to see you.'

Diana nodded and departed, but she could not help feeling a little worried as she returned to the quayside. She hadn't liked the sharp expression in Pollard's eyes! Some deep instinct warned her that Fenton was in a lot more trouble than was evident. Why had Pollard taken Fenton to the police station in the first place? Routine enquiries could easily have been made aboard the schooner. But no doubt the ship had been searched now for signs of Jane Rutherford, and obviously the police had found nothing to prove the girl had ever been aboard.

'What have they charged him with?' Jerry Todd demanded as soon as he saw Diana.

'Jerry,' she retorted in severe tones. 'You let your imagination run away with you. He hasn't been arrested. He's just answering questions.'

'That's the first step,' the pilot retorted. 'He'll be lucky to see the outside of the jail if they don't find the girl.'

'Let's get started or we'll never get done,'

she said with a smile. She felt optimistic about the whole affair. Young girls were forever leaving their homes for hardly any reason at all, and they usually turned up again within a day or two with no apparent harm done. Diana knew Jane well, and would expect the girl to do something hysterical if she became emotional. But there was a small knot of worry in the background of her mind as they set out, and the passing hours did nothing to lessen her tension.

Tuna was a smaller island to the west of St Flavia, and the seaplane covered the watery distance in less than two hours. In that time Diana kept silent, lost in conjecture, and Jerry took her silence as an indication that she was worried. Just before they landed in a lagoon at the island be grinned at her.

'Don't worry, Doctor, a man like Fenton Leigh can take care of himself. He wouldn't do anything foolish.'

'Your imagination is still working overtime, Jerry,' she said with a smile. 'I haven't thought of Fenton Leigh once since we took off. I have my duties to worry about, remember.'

'Of course, Doctor.' He winked at her, and she knew he didn't believe her.

Setting about her work on the island did much to relieve her of her worries, and she was busy enough to occupy two hours of intensive activity. But when they had finished at Tuna and set out for St Lydia, Diana found her thoughts taking control again, and she could not settle back into her former optimism. By the time they reached St Lydia she was trembling inside, certain that the worst that could possibly happen would befall them. She tried to hide her disquiet, but she could see that Jerry was aware of her feelings. He knew that she was no more than an ordinary woman beneath her professional manner, and Fenton Leigh had proved that women could not stand against him. But had that been the case with Jane Rutherford? Suspicion sharpened in Diana's mind, despite her powerful love for Fenton. If any man could turn a girl's head, Fenton could. There just had to be some small grains of truth in all the wild rumours that circulated about him.

In those moments of reflection, Diana found the blackest thoughts, and she knew she was standing at the crossroads in her life. But she could not review the situation impartially. She was too closely involved! Her heart was trying to take over from her head, and she was experienced enough to know that once she let her emotion rule her she was finished . . .

CHAPTER SEVEN

Diana could not help thinking about her previous visit to St Lydia as she worked at the Clinic that afternoon. She tried to lose herself in work, but her feelings were too strong to permit her much peace of mind. But one pleasant surprise was the greater friendliness shown to her by Maria, the nurse. The girl thanked her effusively for sending Andrew Griffith to hospital on St Flavia, and when Diana enquired after the youth's health, the nurse was eager to tell her.

'He will be coming home again in a few days. He tells me the doctor at the hospital said he arrived only in time to save his life. You saved his life, Doctor Brett!'

'That's my job,' Diana said with a pleased smile. Praise like this made all her efforts seem justified.

'It's more than a job with you,' the nurse enthused. 'I know you, Doctor Brett! I've watched the way you work. It doesn't matter to you what the colour of your patient's skin is. You always do your best.'

'I should hope I do,' Diana said, smiling. 'I'm glad Andrew is making progress. It was touch and go, I know, and I hope he will forgive me for lying to him in order to get him to the hospital.'

'He will always be grateful. I spoke to him on the telephone yesterday and he said he had been afraid for nothing. They didn't hurt him.'

'Well, I'm glad he knows that now. He would most certainly have lost his life if we hadn't got him to the hospital.'

'I love him,' Maria said, her breast rising and falling with emotion. 'I want to show you my appreciation in some way. Tell me what I can do, Doctor!'

'There's nothing you can do, Maria. I'm only happy this has turned out right for you and Andrew. A doctor doesn't need thanks for good work. The patient's recovery is more than sufficient thanks.'

'I knew you would look at it like that!' The girl nodded emphatically. 'But I shall watch out for you.'

'Thank you, Maria. That's a comforting thought. Now we'd better get some work done or I shall soon lose my reputation for being a great doctor!' Diana smiled fleetingly.

'I have heard already that trouble is sitting on your shoulder, Doctor!' There was concern in the girl's dusky face, and Diana frowned as she studied the expression.

'What have you heard, Maria? Something about me?'

'About the man you love!'

'What?' Diana was shocked out of her habitual calm. 'About whom are you talking, Maria?'

'Fenton Leigh!'

Diana could only stare at the girl in silent wonder. She had always known that the natives used extraordinary means of communication. At times it didn't seem possible that news could travel so fast and so far even in regions where there were no telephones, but this was impossible. No one outside of Fenton himself had any knowledge of her innermost thoughts.

'Where did you learn this, Maria?' she asked.

The girl was uneasy now, and her dark eyes showed concern. Diana waited, knowing that she had to show patience or lose the chance of learning what she wanted to know.'

'Andrew told me last night, Doctor.'

'What did he tell you?'

'That you and Fenton Leigh are becoming very close!'

'How could Andrew learn that in hospital? I only saw Fenton twice, and nothing could have been gleaned from either of those meetings.' Diana knew Andrew Griffith couldn't possibly have learned about her visit to the boat. She hadn't made the visit until yesterday evening, and that was when Andrew spoke to Maria on the telephone.

'The last time you were on St Lydia.' Maria was watching Diana's face with narrowed brown eyes. 'You were seen, Doctor.'

Diana tried to maintain her expressionless manner, but a light seemed to burst in her mind as she recalled that wonderful moment when Fenton had first taken her into his arms. It had been under the trees on the ridge overlooking the sea. So someone had seen them together! She knew the natives didn't miss anything, but she had thought they were safe from watching eyes in the shadows of the trees.

'No other white person will ever learn of it, Doctor,' Maria said softly. 'You can count on that.'

'I'm sure your people don't gossip half as much as some of mine.' Diana smiled thinly when she thought of Alice Reid. 'But what do you know of Fenton Leigh, Maria?' She glanced at her watch. 'I can spare a few moments, if you have anything interesting to say.'

'What I could tell you would only give you pain,' the girl said quietly, and there was such confidence in her words that Diana suppressed a shiver that threatened to put ice along her spine.

'The truth might hurt, but if there is anything you feel I ought to know then I'd rather you told me. If you do appreciate what I've done for Andrew then tell me, Maria.'

'There is one on St Flavia who would make great mischief for Fenton Leigh,' the girl said in low, vibrant tones. 'I have no need to tell you his name. There are many who talk evil about him, but they have no true knowledge of him and speak only from imagination.'

'But what about Fenton himself? What about him, Maria? Is he the kind of man they say he is?'

'He is the kind of man you need. He has walked many paths around the island, and much of the good that he has done has been forgotten.'

'That's always the case,' Diana said impatiently. 'People usually only remember the bad things.'

'He has done nothing bad!' Maria watched her intently, as if trying to say more with her face than with her lips.

'You would know, you and your people,' Diana said wonderingly. 'What happened to him, Maria? Why has he turned away from everything that he loved?'

'It was written in the fires of long ago,

Doctor.' Maria smiled fleetingly. 'Now I am talking of a subject that clashes with your science, and you have no beliefs in this. I can see by your eyes that you recoil from my words. But we islanders know things that you cannot even begin to understand, and we see much that lies before and after an event.'

'The future,' Diana said slowly. 'You do read the future, Maria.'

'It is forbidden to talk of such matters. I can say no more, but I will warn you, Doctor, that your path lies through dangerous and difficult ways!'

Diana caught her breath. She had never attached much importance to the native beliefs. Her studies led her away from such luxuries. But she knew that many natives built their lives around their own seemingly savage rites and customs, and there were many things which could not be explained.

'Shall we open the clinic now, Doctor?' Maria demanded.

'Yes,' Diana stifled a sigh of impatience. 'I'd better get through here as soon as I can. I want to get back to St Flavia!'

'It isn't on St Flavia where you'll meet your problems,' Maria said, and Diana was flabbergasted, but when she tried to get more from the nurse, Maria refused to speak.

Seeing nine patients didn't help Diana's

mind at all, and by the time she was ready to start her round of the white people she was filled with a strange sense of anticipation. She believed what Maria had told her. There was trouble looming up over the horizon for her! She knew that without having to be told. She had known it instinctively from the first moment she realized that she loved Fenton! But she was prepared to face anything in order to keep her love. She knew it was not just a momentary flash of passion that would burn itself out through its own intensity. Although she had never been in love before she knew this was the real thing, and her instincts proved it to her.

It was late afternoon before she was ready to return to the clinic, and she had a headache, brought on mainly by the torrent of fears raising themselves in her avid mind. When she saw Jerry waiting patiently near the seaplane she felt a mounting of relief in her breast, and as soon as she had finished her last-minute work she took her leave of Maria and prepared to return to St Flavia.

'Been busy, Doctor?' Jerry demanded as he took her medical bag.

'As usual,' she replied, getting into the cockpit. She gave a long sigh as she settled down and strapped herself in. 'I shan't be sorry to get back to St Flavia!'

'It won't take us long!' He gave her a hard, long look, and quickly prepared for take-off. As they soared into the bright sky Diana felt some of her mood slip away from her. She was letting her imagination run riot, she told herself, hunching forward to watch the island disappear. Ahead of them stretched the sea, and they were flying north-east.

As they reached the halfway mark, Jerry tilted the starboard wing a little and pointed down to the surface of the sea.

'There's Skull Rock!'

'Yes! I always look at it as we pass over.' Diana stared at the unusual rock breaking the smooth surface below. It was several hundred yards in diameter, completely bare except for an ancient temple that had been built upon it by natives many generations before. The temple was in ruins now, and overgrown with vegetation that abounded the small area. The rest of the island was bare rock, poking up out of the blue sea like a human skull. Diana had visited it once, and had been overpowered by her feelings that something was wrong with the place. She had heard that it was still used by natives who practised voodoo, but no one else, not even fishermen, went there.

'One day we'll drop down there for a visit, when you have some time to spare,' Jerry said, and Diana suppressed a shudder.

'No thanks,' she retorted. 'It isn't my idea of a picnic site.'

He grinned and they went on, the island slipping away beneath them. Diana kept glancing down at it until she could see it no longer, and she remembered her fears on that bright afternoon she had visited it years before. It had been so lonely, so desolate! Standing on the bare rock on top of the vertical cliffs, she had imagined those past generations of natives who had practised their dark rites there, and it seemed to her that some of their tremendous mental power had remained to taint the very rock.

She was still musing about her unknown fears when they reached St Flavia, and the sight of Fenton's schooner down there in the bay caused her to wonder what had happened to him. She had been hoping against hope that Jane Rutherford would turn up unscathed and with a very ordinary excuse for her disappearance, but whatever happened to the girl, Diana was certain Fenton had nothing to do with her disappearance.

They touched down upon the water and sent spray flying through the air. But Diana had eyes only for the schooner, and she saw the Polynesian, Zero, standing on the deck, watching their machine intently. There was no sign of anyone else aboard, and Diana felt a pang of worry as she imagined that Fenton himself was still at the police station under suspicion of something or other.

'There you are, Doctor,' Jerry said as he helped her out of the plane. 'See you tomorrow, eh?'

'Yes. It will probably be Sama and Tope tomorrow, Jerry.'

'It's all the same to me!' He grinned at her. 'I suppose you will be interested in what's been happening here today, though. Do you reckon they're still holding Leigh?'

'I have no idea.' Diana could not contain her anxiety.

'We'll soon know,' Jerry grinned as he turned his attention to his plane.

Diana stared at him for a moment, then went off, and she walked quickly along the quay, intending to fetch her car and drive home. She dearly wanted to go out to the schooner, but was afraid to excite any comment upon her actions. Word would get out as it was that she had been aboard the previous evening until almost midnight, and she couldn't help wondering what some of her patients might have to say about that. Not that they would say anything to her face, but people like Mrs Reid would make capital out of the incident.

As she passed the police station a voice

called to her, and she paused and looked back to see Inspector Pollard standing at the window.

'If you can spare a moment, Doctor,' he said. 'I know you must be very tired after your long day, but I won't keep you long.'

'Certainly, Inspector!' She tried to show a carefree face, but knew that she failed. She entered the building and the Inspector came to meet her, ushering her into his office. He pulled forward a seat for her and Diana sat down. 'Not going to hold me for questioning, are you?' she demanded.

'I'm not holding anyone,' he retorted, moving to his desk and seating himself. He studied her for a moment, his grey eyes cold and sparkling, and Diana found herself relieved that she had not lied to him. 'I've been pursuing my enquiries all day,' he went on at length. 'I've established that Fenton Leigh was not the last person to see Jane Rutherford on the quayside, and there is no evidence to suggest what may have happened to her. She hasn't reappeared yet!'

'What do you think has happened to her, Inspector?'

'In my job it's better not to hazard guesses, Doctor. You wouldn't guess a diagnosis, would you? You get all the facts you can to make a picture, and from that picture, however incomplete it may be, you make your diagnosis. Well that's near enough the way I work. I don't take into consideration what the gossips say. I know for a fact that Fenton Leigh has never given us any trouble involving women. That's all I have to work on. The fact that you were with him all last evening goes a long way to convince me that he didn't see Jane Rutherford again after leaving her on the quay.'

'Why did she speak to him?' Diana tried to keep her tones casual, but there was a harshness in her throat which sounded in her words.

'It seems she wanted passage off St Flavia!' Pollard smiled. 'I believe him. He told her he wasn't sailing away. That was the end of it as far as Leigh was concerned. I think it's the truth, but I expect all the gossips on the island are concocting a far different tale.'

'Have you seen Geoff Foster yet, Inspector?'

'No. I'm going out to your place later this evening. Will you be there if I should require to see you?'

'I don't know.' Diana shook her head slowly. 'It all depends. You know I get called out on a case very frequently.'

'That's all right. I don't suppose I shall need to take a formal statement from you. This information doesn't affect my investigations, although I shall keep it in mind. I thought you would like to know that Leigh is not suspected of anything.'

'Thank you, Inspector!' Diana smiled, and relief was large inside her.

'Leigh isn't a bad fellow, you know. I was on the case that time he got into trouble. He did what he thought was best for the patient. It wasn't exactly proved that he killed the patient to end his misery, but he was extremely careless. I suppose you come across borderline cases like that, don't you, Doctor?'

'I do.' Diana nodded slowly. 'I sometimes wonder why I have to try and keep life in a body when it would be better for the patient to die.'

'I get the same sort of thing with some of the criminals I deal with. I sometimes wish I could let a man go free. Not that I ever do. The law is the law. But it is pretty easy to run up against the law when you're dealing with people. The law is black and white in its interpretation of the facts, but people are human, and it's hard sometimes to equate one with the other.'

'I understand, Inspector. Thank you for calling me in. It has relieved my mind considerably.' Diana took her leave and went on, her step lighter, her shoulders square. She had a feeling that Fenton would bring his ship round to the cove in time to meet her that evening, and her heart leaped with wild hope as she imagined herself in his arms.

She went home to change, having to be back in town for her evening surgery, and as the time went by her anticipation increased until she was nervous and trembling. But her sublime happiness was marred by thoughts of the missing girl. Why had Jane Rutherford chosen this particular time to disappear?

For the first time in her career, Diana found surgery a bore! It shocked her to realize that she wasn't really listening to her patients! Her mind was throbbing with thoughts of Fenton when she ought to be concentrating upon her work. It was a bad sign! She tried to snap out of it, but her attitude towards Fenton was such that nothing else was powerful enough to compete successfully. She was crazily in love with a comparative stranger! The thought held her for some time. But a part of her mind objected strenuously. Fenton was not a stranger! He had never been a stranger!

But she was shaken from her thoughts when she rang for her next patient and Alice Reid appeared in the doorway.

'Hello, Doctor!' Alice Reid never called Diana by her name when she was visiting as a patient, and Diana was pleased by the arrangement. It told her in advance if she could expect to treat the woman or would get some unwanted gossip. At one time Mrs Reid had come to the surgery and taken her turn with the other patients, just to impart some snippet of scandal she had picked up, but Diana had taught her better since those early days.

'What's wrong, Mrs Reid?' Diana stiffened in her seat despite her control. With Fenton in the forefront of her mind, and so much speculation going the rounds about him, she had every right to fear that this woman had gleaned some information from somewhere.

'I have headaches more frequently these days, Doctor. I would like something for them.'

'Do you wear glasses at all?' Diana had to force her mind to concentrate upon what she was saying. Her mind was thrusting up pictures of Fenton as he had stood upon the deck of his schooner the first afternoon she had met him. There were mysterious little thrills pattering through her breast, and she noticed that her fingers were trembling as she clasped them on the desk before her.

'Only for reading. You were saying the last time I called that I might need glasses all the time.'

'Perhaps we'd better send you to see Mr Wagner!' Diana prepared to fill out a form. 'Go along and see him and he will test your sight.'

'Thank you, I will. But perhaps you'll give me something for the pain.'

'I will.' Diana took up her prescription pad. She had a feeling that when this particular business was closed Mrs Reid would attempt to broach other subjects, and she wanted to get rid of her as quickly as possible. If there were other patients waiting then it wouldn't be too difficult, but Diana had the feeling that Mrs Reid sat in the waiting room until she was the last patient, and her spirits sank as the woman, taking the prescription, said:

'I'm the last one this evening, Diana. I'm glad, because I want to talk to you.'

'Not now, Mrs Reid, if you don't mind. It's been a hard day and I'm very tired. I have a headache, too.'

'I think you ought to listen to what I have to say!' Mrs Reid's dark eyes snapped a little as she blinked furiously, her steady gaze holding Diana's eyes against her will.

'I suppose it's about Fenton Leigh!' Diana sighed wearily knowing from experience that it would be easier to listen than to try and get away.

'No!'

'Not Fenton?' Diana showed surprise. 'You were really ripping him to pieces last evening, Mrs Reid.'

'Only because I thought he was guilty of something.'

'And now you don't?' Diana was definitely interested.

'I wouldn't say for certain, but I've discovered that there was a man in Jane Rutherford's life.'

'Really? Who?' Diana was a little disappointed.

'Your father's manager, Geoff Foster! Didn't you know he's been seeing Jane Rutherford on the odd evening lately?'

'No I didn't, and I fail to see why that should arouse interest.' Diana was ready to call a halt. This was the usual thing. She had hoped to learn something of the situation surrounding the missing girl, but Alice Reid was interested only in the gossip value, and Diana realized that she ought to have known better than hope for something really interesting from this woman.

'Didn't Jane visit you as a patient a few weeks ago?'

'I have seen her recently,' Diana admitted. 'What are you getting at?'

'I think she was in trouble.' There was sharp eagerness now in Mrs Reid's voice.

'With a man?' Diana smiled and shook her head. 'You're trying too hard to rattle skeletons, Mrs Reid. Jane didn't consult me on any such matter.'

'I'm sure she didn't, because she lost her nerve at the last moment. She wanted to, no doubt, because she must have been getting frantic. That's why she's disappeared! She's probably done away with herself!'

'I think you're going a bit too far this time, Mrs Reid.' Diana got to her feet and walked to the door, her tones indicating that the matter was closed. 'I don't know what poor Mrs Rutherford would say if she heard this sort of thing. She must be dreadfully upset as it is by her daughter's disappearance. I feel it is my duty to warn you that this kind of talk is highly dangerous, and if you have any sense at all you wouldn't repeat it.'

'I have no intention of repeating it!' Alice Reid sounded highly indignant. 'I mention this to you because you are a doctor, and I feel that someone ought to know what the true situation really is. I'm certain I'm right. I've heard about a conversation that took place between Jane and Geoffrey Foster the other evening.'

'Then I suggest you call on Inspector Pollard and give him the information. There's nothing I can do about it.'

Mrs Reid sighed heavily and came towards the door. She paused when she drew level with Diana, and her dark eyes were narrowed, filled with the determined light that Diana knew so well.

'You'll see that I'm right, when events come to light, but it will be too late to help that poor girl then. Something should be done about it now, in case there's still a chance that she's alive.'

Diana shook her head and Mrs Reid stifled a sigh and departed. Going back to her desk, Diana rang for the next patient, but the receptionist entered and told her that Mrs Reid had been the last one. Diana nodded and relaxed. Her first instinct was to hurry home and prepare for the evening, but she could not overlook what Mrs Reid had said. She tapped her fingers upon the desk while she considered the thoughts the woman's words had brought into prominence. But she couldn't believe that Geoffrey Foster was involved with Jane Rutherford. Any man but Geoff! He just was not the type!

She gathered together her things and prepared to leave, but when she reached the door she paused and turned to stare at the telephone. A few timely words might well save someone a lot of grief! The thought was firm in her mind, and Diana sighed as she went back to the desk. She called Inspector Pollard, and stumbled through an explanation of what she had learned. She didn't like this at all. It was too much like repeating gossip, but she was surprised when the Inspector thanked her warmly.

'I've been looking for a hidden lead in this case,' he said. 'I think this may be it. You didn't learn the nature of that conversation Jane had with Foster, did you?'

'No! I shut the woman up. I dislike gossip intensely, Inspector.'

'Of course, but sometimes it pays to listen. However I shall look into this. I'm at my wits end, to tell you the truth. The girl simply vanished without trace. You've been most helpful to me today, Doctor.'

Diana hung up, a little pensive now, and as she drove homeward she couldn't help wondering about the future and where her happiness would fit into it. She could only hope!

CHAPTER EIGHT

Geoffrey Foster was waiting for Diana when she reached home, and she caught her breath at sight of him, for her mind had been weaving dark pictures about his supposed secret affairs with Jane Rutherford. But she greeted him politely, too painfully aware of the incidents of the previous night.

'Diana, I must talk to you,' he said worriedly. 'Can you spare me a few moments?'

She looked into his face and saw genuine worry there, and that was unusual for him. She fancied that what had happened last night was preying on his mind, but his degree of worry seemed out of all proportion.

'Aren't you feeling well, Geoff?' she demanded, getting out of her car.

'I'm feeling all right, but I'd like to talk to you.'

'Well we're alone here!' She glanced around the yard. Her mother was standing at a window, watching them, it seemed to Diana. But there was no one within earshot.

'Not here,' he begged. 'Meet me later, will you?'

'I can't do that. You'll have to talk to me here.'

'You're going to see Fenton Leigh this evening?' His eyes darkened slightly and his brows drew together.

'That's none of your business, Geoff, and I want you to understand that. I won't tolerate any interference from you. I am quite old enough to know what I'm doing.'

'I'm only thinking of you, Diana,' he said slowly. 'I'd hate for you to walk into a lot of grief when a few timely words from me might save you.'

She tensed as she realized that she had used the same excuse to talk to Inspector Pollard, and she was reminded of Maria's words, back there on St Lydia, about dangers and difficulties coming her way. Maria had spoken from her heart, because of her deep appreciation for what she had done for Andrew Griffith. Ice seemed to pack around Diana's heart as she stared into his face. He seemed so serious!

'What's on your mind, Geoff?' she demanded.

'You, naturally! I am concerned about your future. I know you're going to think that I'm just jealous of Fenton Leigh, but you know I do love you, and I wouldn't do anything to hurt you. I love you enough to step aside if I thought you would find happiness with Leigh. But I know you're making a bad mistake, Diana, and I will do anything to prevent tragedy. You're not like an ordinary woman. Scandal can be shrugged aside by a lesser person, but your work is your whole life, and it would finish you if something ever happened to take medicine away from you.'

'I don't understand, Geoff! What is it you know about Fenton that's so terrible? What kind of a man is he that I will lose everything just by knowing him?'

'How can one put it into so many words? He was struck off the medical register, and he'll see to it that the same thing happens to you. He's malicious and shallow, and he has no scruples at all where any woman is concerned.'

Diana shook her head as she listened. She was thinking of what he might be guilty of, with Jane Rutherford, and it was in her to blurt out what she had heard, but she knew she might jeopardize the Inspector's case by saying anything.

'You're not giving me facts, just your own impressions, Geoff,' she said slowly. 'You don't know Fenton yourself. How can you say what he'll do? You're giving your imagination too much scope. You're wasting my time with this nonsense, and I'm getting very short of patience after your high-handed ways last night.'

He stared at her, his face tight, closed against her, then he shook his head. 'You've changed already, Diana,' he said. 'In the very short time you've known Leigh, you've changed! That should be warning enough.'

'We all change, Geoff. Even you! Looking

at you now, I can see that you're not exactly the kind of man I thought you were!' She shook her head impatiently and stepped around him. 'I think we'll get along much better if you forget about me. I have my life to lead and you have more than enough on your plate. What's worrying you, anyway? There is something else on your mind. You didn't sleep too well last night, did you?'

'What do you expect?' he demanded in bitter tones. 'I found the woman I love in another man's arms. To cap that, he is the most undesirable man in the islands.'

Diana did not reply, but walked away, carrying her medical bag as if it were suddenly too heavy for her. She saw her mother still at the window, and frowned a little as she sensed that there was something else amiss! Her instincts warned her that she could expect some trouble, especially if Alice Reid had picked up the news about Diana's visit to the police station this morning, and the reasons for it.

Entering the house, Diana quickly found that her intuition had been correct. Mrs Brett came from the lounge and stood in the doorway, watching Diana in the hall as she set down her bag. When Diana looked at her mother, Mrs Brett took her gaze elsewhere for a moment, then looked at Diana again.

'Before you take a shower, dear, I'd like to have a chat with you.'

'Certainly, Mother. What's wrong?'

'Come in here!' Mrs Brett moved back from the doorway of the lounge and Diana entered, filled with reluctance, fearing that this chat might touch upon her own personal life. But that would depend upon the informant who had reached her mother. If Geoff had said anything about the previous evening! Her face stiffened at the thought. But more likely it would have been Alice Reid.

'Well?' Diana was aware that she showed defiance, and her tones were so harsh her voice sounded unnatural even to her own ears.

'You're expecting trouble from me!' Mrs Brett came across the room to confront Diana. 'You know what I'm going to talk about.'

'I assure you, Mother, that I have no idea what's in your mind. I can tell that it's serious, but that's all.'

'It is serious. Doctor Hamilton telephoned me this afternoon and acquainted me with certain information regarding your activities last night. When I had recovered from the shock he told me to warn you to be careful.'

'I see!' Diana's lips thinned as she took a deep breath. 'Exactly what did Doctor Hamilton tell you about last night?'

'Do I have to repeat it?'

'Certainly! I have no doubt it's a pack of lies, or wishful thinking stirred up by malicious tongues that should be better employed.'

'Doctor Hamilton is your superior, Diana, and he's very worried about your reputation.'

'Then he should mind his own business and let me worry about my own reputation.'

'I have the feeling that what he told me is partly true! I have never seen you in this attitude before! I had a word with Geoffrey this morning, after Doctor Hamilton called, and he confirmed some of the facts I learned over the telephone.'

'Mother, unless you tell me exactly what you heard then I cannot say what's true or not.'

Mrs Brett sighed heavily, then began to outline the incidents which had taken place the previous night. Diana nodded to herself as she listened. The basic facts were true, but someone had done some verbal embroidery. When her mother fell silent and stared at her with mute accusation in her pale blue eyes, Diana took a deep breath.

'Mother, you have the facts, but quite a lot has been added to them. I certainly haven't done anything to be ashamed of, and what happened last night is my business, anyway. I don't know why you should upset yourself about this. I'm thirty-two years old, not sixteen!'

'It's not myself I'm worried for, it's you! Can't you see what scandal will do to your reputation? Doctor Hamilton is already concerned about this. I don't have to tell you how strict they are! You could lose your job, and perhaps your right to practise!'

'Did Doctor Hamilton say as much?' Diana was trying hard to prevent her heart lurching with mental sickness. But she knew deep in her heart that she would not, could not, forget about Fenton. Such was the power he exercised over her that she was prepared to forget about her family and her way of life! The knowledge came through to her as she studied her mother's face, and it shocked and confused her. How could she consider placing everything she had worked for in jeopardy for a man she hardly knew? But she loved him. She breathed love for him! She was twisted and pinioned by it. She loved Fenton Leigh and nothing she did could change it.

'Doctor Hamilton said many things, and they all added up to the same thing.' Mrs Brett spoke unusually harshly. 'Diana, I implore you to forget this madness!'

'Madness?' Diana was struggling against the part of her mind controlling thoughts of Fenton. Her saner self was telling her that this was madness! She could instinctively divine that the course she was choosing would lead into tumultuous waters, and she recalled Maria's words about dangers and difficulties waiting in the future for her. 'I don't know what you mean, Mother. How can it be madness to know a man?'

'A man like Fenton Leigh! He's under suspicion now of having something to do with Jane Rutherford's disappearance. Why couldn't you choose a man like Geoffrey? He's quiet and responsible. He's never caused any trouble, and he simply adores you.'

'I don't have any feelings for Geoffrey. I've told him that! And Fenton Leigh is almost a stranger to me, so I don't see what all the fuss is about.'

'One doesn't have to know Fenton long to feel the effects of his personality.'

'Mother, this is ridiculous! I've been around these islands as a doctor for just over four years now, and I've met everyone and been everywhere. A doctor is supposed to be above reproach. I admit that what happened last evening was a little unusual, but surely I've managed to build up a reputation while I've been practising here!'

'People only believe what they want to believe! You must never forget that, Diana. It would be a tragedy if you did something foolish now and ruined your whole life. You must see that having a friendship with Fenton Leigh is definitely a disadvantage.'

'I see nothing of the kind, and I'll tell anyone who is interested the same thing. I find this discussion distasteful, Mother. I will not be dictated to about my personal life.'

'I can see why every woman is afraid of Fenton Leigh,' Mrs Brett said sorrowfully. 'Even a girl like you has been bewitched by him.'

'It's nothing of the sort, Mother, and you know it.' Diana shook her head. If her mother took this attitude then what could she expect from other people? What capital would Mrs Reid make from the news that the island doctor was spending time in the company of the most notorious man they had in the area? But Fenton was nothing of the kind! People had given him a name and they were not giving him a chance to prove himself otherwise. She suppressed a sigh and glanced at her watch. 'Look, I want to go out this evening, and it's getting late. I've had a very busy day. I'm not in the mood for a lecture of this kind, Mother.'

'Don't take it like that, Diana. I'm not lecturing you! I'm only looking at the situation from a detached angle. I can see the dangers where you can't. It's all very well saying you are adult! We all know that. You've proved it in the last four years. But you are in a profession where the slightest breath of scandal can do irreparable harm. Think of your future life, Diana. I can assure you that Doctor Hamilton feels his board will frown most severely upon this strange friendship you're forming. It wouldn't take much for the committee to make some drastic decision. What would you do if you lost this job?'

'Don't be absurd, Mother!' Diana shook her head. 'Look, I'm sorry for sounding a bit short, but it has been hectic today, and I don't like the thought of everyone on the islands poking their noses into my business. If Fenton Leigh is supposed to be such a bad hat then why isn't he in jail? How is it he's never been in jail?'

'I know your loyalties are strong, and I'm proud of you for being so, but you must consider your work, Diana!'

'I've done nothing but that, and to the best of my ability, since as long as I can remember.' Diana smiled. 'I'm not concerned about the chatter of a few busybodies, Mother. My work stands by results, and that's good enough for me.'

The telephone rang and Diana turned away to answer it, but Mrs Brett beat her to the instrument and lifted it quickly to her ear. Diana watched her mother's face, half expecting the call to be for her. She was called out on emergencies sometimes, and that involved a quick air dash to one or another of the islands. But this time it was not as she expected. Mrs Brett lowered the telephone and covered the mouthpiece with her hand.

'It's Fenton Leigh,' she said in hollow tones.

'Well give me the phone!' Diana held out her hand for it.

'Wait a moment!' Her mother showed unusual determination. She lifted the receiver to her ear again. 'Mr Leigh, Diana is at home and she is preparing to go out this evening, no doubt to see you.'

Diana nodded slowly, and Mrs Brett shook her head ruefully. Diana reached for the telephone, but her mother moved away.

'If you want to see Diana perhaps you would call here for her. I would like to have a chat with you, Mr. Leigh.'

Diana suppressed a sigh. This situation was ludicrous! She could almost see the funny side of it. Perhaps Mrs Reid would organize a Save the Doctor march through Tenka! She smiled at the thought, and watched her mother's face as Mrs Brett replaced the telephone receiver.

'And what have you arranged on my behalf, Mother?'

'He'll come here to pick you up, and I would like a few moments alone with him, Diana.'

'You're just thinking of your motherly duties, no doubt.' Diana smiled slowly. 'All right, Mother, but don't be too old fashioned in your approach to him or he may laugh at you. In fact, I feel like laughing right now. What's supposed to be wrong with Fenton, anyway? Has he some dire disease that's deadly dangerous to women?'

'Don't joke, Diana. Think of Jane Rutherford.'

'I've been thinking of that girl all day.' Diana sobered and a frown touched her face. 'Inspector Pollard doesn't think Fenton is guilty of anything, and he ought to know!'

She turned away before her mother could attempt to prolong their talk, and she went up to her room to prepare for the evening. Her thoughts were clearer as she imagined Fenton coming to the door. She wanted to see him in her home! She didn't think anything her mother had to say would make the slightest difference to what Fenton already thought about the situation. He must be well used to being warned off by anxious parents!

But Diana was feeling tired as she

showered, then dressed in a thin silk blouse and short cotton skirt. She stayed in her room, not wanting to reopen that discussion with her mother, and when she heard a car in the yard outside she peered from the window in time to see Fenton alighting. Her heart seemed to miss a beat at sight of him. She smiled tenderly as her searching eyes took in every detail of his powerful figure. He was dressed in a pale blue lightweight suit, with a white nylon shirt open at the top button. There was a cravat knotted at his throat, and he looked thoroughly masculine and attractive.

He glanced around for a moment, then stiffened, and Diana followed the direction of his gaze and saw Geoffrey Foster standing on the verandah in front of his bungalow. But as Fenton glanced at him, Geoff turned and entered the low building, and Diana shook her head slowly as she recognized the stiff set of Geoff's shoulders. There would be trouble between those two yet! The thought shivered through her mind. Was it this situation to which Maria had been alluding when she had issued her warning?

When Fenton moved towards the door of the house Diana's first instinct was to rush down and greet him, but she realized that her mother wanted to say something to him, and if she didn't get the chance she might be all the more troublesome later. Fenton would take it all in good part. He didn't seem to let anything worry him!

Diana gave her mother ten minutes, then went down to the lounge, and she paused at the door, hearing voices inside. She took a deep breath and forced up an attitude of casualness she was far from feeling. Then she opened the door and swept into the room.

Fenton got to his feet from a seat by the open window, and Diana saw that her mother was looking slightly harassed. Mrs Brett had been in the middle of a sentence, but she broke off at Diana's entrance and got to her feet. As Fenton came forward to greet Diana, her mother moved to the door.

'Thank you for being patient with me, Mr Leigh,' Mrs Brett said. 'I trust I didn't bore you.'

'On the contrary, Mrs Brett. You entertained me tremendously. I hope we shall meet again.'

Diana's mother smiled gently and departed, casting a sidelong glance at Diana which was supposed to convey some message, but Diana could make nothing of it, and she stood watching her mother until the door of the room closed hesitantly behind her.

'I've been getting a lecture,' Fenton said

slowly, his eyes impassive as he stared into Diana's face.

'Part of the one that was awaiting me when I arrived home,' she said. 'What sort of a man are you, Fenton, that mothers should fear for their daughters at the very mention of your name?'

He smiled, but did not reply. She looked into his face, trying to discover what it was about him that attracted her so powerfully. Her heart was erratic for a few moments, and she sighed when she failed to pinpoint his attractiveness. There was nothing she could put her finger on. It was all of him! Everything about him appealed to her, and she tried to steady herself, hoping against hope that she was not making a mistake, but something seemed to tell her that even if she were, and she knew it, she would be powerless to do anything decisive about it.

'Mothers have a special duty towards their daughters, and I'm pleased to see that your mother takes her duties seriously. I'm glad she intends keeping a close eye on my activities. I never know when I shall need a good witness. But before we go any further, Diana, I want to tell you how much I appreciate what you did for me today. I might have been in a pretty awkward position if you hadn't volunteered that information. Thank you for trying to save my skin at the risk of your reputation.'

'What really happened yesterday?' she demanded. 'You saw Jane Rutherford, didn't you?'

'So they say. I wouldn't know. But I do remember a girl of the description the Inspector gave me coming up to me on the quay. She must have seen me rowing ashore from the ship. She asked me if I was sailing from the island soon, and when I said no she disappeared.'

'She certainly disappeared, Fenton.' Diana shook her head as she failed to find any light in the long black stretch of her thoughts.

'The Inspector will find her if anyone can,' he said, looking into her face with critical eyes. 'But what about you, Diana? From what your mother says, I imagine you're going to be in a lot of trouble through knowing me.'

'I don't see why!' She stared at him, trying to read his mind, but his handsome face was impassive, his sharp brown eyes narrowed and bright.

'Your mother says Doctor Hamilton has been in touch with her already about your activities last night. Aren't you concerned that you may lose your position here? I thought you were keen on medicine!'

'You know I am, Fenton, but I don't see why I can't know you as well! What's supposed to be wrong with you?'

'It's nothing to do with my physical self! It's something inside me which they see.'

'And what's that?' she prompted.

'I've got a black soul!' He smiled thinly. 'That's how it was described to me. Can you imagine it? I'm tainted by the Devil!'

'That's nonsense!' Diana shook her head disgustedly. 'You're joking, Fenton!'

'I wish to God I were!' He sounded deadly serious. 'At first it was like a joke to me! Apart from losing my way of life! That really shook me! When I was no longer a doctor I felt as if I were a son of Satan!'

'Don't talk like that,' she commanded.

'Can you imagine how you would feel if they took away your right to practise medicine?'

'Yes!' Diana suppressed a shudder. 'It would be dreadful.'

'Then why are you so intent upon seeing me, knowing that you run the risk of getting thrown out of medical circles? Your mother has warned you of this possibility, she told me so.'

'Perhaps I'd rather lose my work than you!' She stared into his face with a challenge showing in her eyes, and he shook his head slowly, his face turning grave.

'Diana, how can you be sure after such a short time?'

'How can you ask that, Fenton?' she countered.

'You say you haven't been in love before. How do you know this is the real thing?'

'Because instinct tells me. If I would rather lose my work than you then obviously I am in love with you.'

'The great disadvantage about love is that it destroys all sense of values.'

'That's a cynical outlook!' she retorted.

'But very true, and I can see it where you can't.'

'What's all this leading up to, Fenton? Surely you haven't let my mother's words get through to you!'

'I have, Diana. I've been in this position before. Your position, I mean. I thought at the time that being barred from medicine wasn't the end of the world. I was wrong. As the months went by I realized that I had lost the most precious thing in my life. From my own experiences I can tell that you will come to the same decision eventually. You love me now, but in six months you will realize that medicine does come first in your life, and you will begin to hate me! You'll end up hating everybody, as I almost did, and then you're going to find that your life is completely ruined!'

'Never!' The word quivered on her lips.

'I know I'm right.' His tones had hardened suddenly. 'I'm going to prove to you just how much I love you, Diana! I'm going away this evening and I shall never come back to the islands.'

'No!' She pushed herself into his arms. 'Fenton, tell me you love me, that you want me! Nothing else matters but our love!'

'No!' His tones were suddenly final. 'I'm not going to risk hurting you. It would finish me to know that I had ruined your life. My duty is clear. I'm going, and nothing you can say will stop me. Goodbye, Diana! Go on with your good work.'

He turned abruptly, pushing away her clutching hands, and he walked from the room with determined strides. Diana stared after him, too shocked by his apparently sudden decision. There was a pang in her breast and ice formed in her brain, freezing her thoughts, stunning her with fear. Then she caught her breath and started to the door after him. She hurried out to the verandah and saw him getting into the car, and before she could catch him he drove away viciously, spraying dirt across the yard with his churning wheels.

Diana paused in the yard, dust drifting into her face, and she watched his progress until he was lost to sight beyond a bend in the narrow road. Her spirits sank slowly to zero and her whole world seemed to totter and crumble. Suddenly her legs seemed to lose their strength and her whole body weakened. She stared into the distance, hoping against hope that he would suddenly return, and she was unaware that Geoff Foster was watching her from his bungalow.

Then resistance flared inside her and she started to her feet. There were no problems for her! She didn't care so much about medicine, and that left her free for Fenton. Running to her car, she climbed in and started off in pursuit. Love was motivating her. Love was the most powerful emotion in the world, and in her breast was a gnawing hunger for this wonderful, powerful man who had shown her how to love. She had to get to him! She needed him more than anything in the world!

CHAPTER NINE

Diana was frantic as she drove into Tenka. Her mind was fixed upon Fenton, and she wanted to get to him, to try and convince him that he was wrong. She was prepared to do anything to prove to him that their love was all that mattered, and she drove recklessly on the narrow road, completely out of character for the first time in her life. Something strange inside her, burning and terrible, was pushing her to distraction. She could think of nothing but her passion for Fenton. He had awakened strange and powerful instincts inside her, and she would throw up life itself to be with him.

Twice she almost ran off the road on the bends that came up, and fear lay inside her like a serpent, but she went on, afraid that Fenton would leave before she could catch him. Then she became aware that a car was coming along very fast behind her, and she narrowed her eyes when she recognized it as Geoff Foster's. Her lips compressed as she saw that he was overtaking her, and she fancied that he had overheard her conversation with Fenton and wanted to stop her. No doubt he was in league with her mother! The thought pushed her even further from sanity.

But as fast as she was driving, Foster managed to creep up beside her, and he waved frantically for her to stop when she looked at him. She shook her head, forcing him well out into the road, and he had to brake sharply and pull in behind her when a car appeared from the opposite direction. Before he could catch up with her again they were in the outskirts of the town, and Diana slowed the car and drove towards the quay. Foster kept close behind her, and Diana gritted her teeth as she stared ahead.

When she reached the waterfront Diana saw Fenton in the rowing boat, pulling strongly towards his schooner, and she stopped the car and leaped out, running to the water's edge and looking around frantically for a boatman to take her out to the ship. But the next moment Foster arrived, leaping out of his car and running to her side.

'Have you gone crazy?!' he demanded, seizing her by the shoulder and spinning her around to face him. She saw that he was carrying her medical bag. 'Why the devil didn't you stop on the road when I caught up with you?'

'No one is going to stop me doing anything I want,' she retorted.

'The heat must be affecting your brain,' he snapped. 'I came to tell you that there was an emergency call for you. There's been an accident on Tara! You're needed there immediately. The seaplane is waiting for you. Look!' He pointed along the quay, and Diana caught her breath when she saw Jerry Todd at the side of the small plane, prepared for take-off. 'You were out of your mind on that road,' Foster went on angrily. 'What's happened to you, Diana?'

'Say what you like, Geoff. It will make no difference.' She stared after the small boat that Fenton was rowing. He had almost reached the ship now. She held her breath as she took her bag from Geoff, then her pent up breath escaped her in a long, bitter sigh. Without another word she turned and hurried along the quay to where Jerry Todd stood waiting. He was grinning as she approached him.

'You've broken all records this time,' he said.

'Have you the details of this emergency?' she demanded through stiff lips.

'Yes. There's been a nasty accident on Tara. Three men have been badly injured.'

'Are they sending the special helicopter to bring them in to the hospital?' Diana handed her bag to him and climbed into the cockpit.

'It's out on a job now. A ship is in difficulties off Sama. That's why we have to go. Those injured men need urgent medical attention.'

Diana said no more, and took her bag from him as he handed it up. She sat staring at the schooner as Jerry made his last minute preparations and then he joined her in the cockpit. She glanced along the quay and saw Geoffrey standing by his car. Her breathing seemed to die on her, and she sat completely motionless for some fleeting seconds. When the powerful engine roared into life she drew a sharp breath, and the sound of her sigh was lost in the vibrating noise that filled the cockpit.

Jerry took off quickly, and Diana stared down at the motionless schooner until it was lost to sight under their tail. Then she relaxed slightly, and the coldness around her heart closed in a little tighter and set like ice. She stared ahead unseeingly, silent and tense. She would never see Fenton again! The knowledge was cold certainty in her bemused mind. There seemed to be a sinking feeling in her breast, and tears were lying behind her eyes.

Her thoughts were following a narrow track through the centre of her brain, and the main avenue seemed to lead straight into the black pit of despair that had opened up inside her at Fenton's last words. She had lost him! She had fallen in love with him at first sight, and for a few unbelievable days she had lived on the apex of ecstasy. Now it was all over, like a beautiful dream that dies when faced with sharp reality. Her work stood between them. She had thought it wouldn't! She had felt that their love was strong enough to withstand any shock. But Fenton had known better! That's why he had departed so suddenly.

He had known that nothing could come of their hopes, and her action of departing on this emergency flight proved to her beyond all doubt that she had to do that for which she had been trained. She was a doctor and her duty came first!

They reached Tara quickly, and Diana saw a little knot of people waiting by the landing place. Heaving a long sigh, she dragged herself from her thoughts and prepared herself mentally for what lay ashore. Jerry set down the plane in the dying light of evening, and spray flew across the windshield as they skimmed like a gigantic bird over the smooth surface of the water.

'I'd better come with you, hadn't I?' Jerry demanded as she climbed stiffly from the plane, and Diana nodded as she turned to face the reception committee. She didn't know what to expect, and might need help at the scene of the accident.

The island policeman was waiting for them with a jeep, and Diana pushed her way to his side through the clamouring people all trying to tell her what had happened. The policeman shouted for order and the crowd fell silent. In sharp tones he told Diana what had happened.

'We have three men in the Clinic, Doctor. They stole a car and sped around the island, but the driver lost control and they went over a cliff. I fear for the lives of two of them!'

'Take me to the Clinic quickly,' Diana ordered. She climbed into the jeep and they waited for Jerry to join them. The crowd began to follow along behind as the powerful little vehicle jerked forward and then sped along.

The Clinic was a tin hut set on the edge of the main village, and there was an even larger crowd standing outside its narrow door. The people scattered as the jeep came up, and a confused chattering started as Diana alighted and hurried into the building. Now her worries were forgotten. Her mind lost all thoughts of her personal self, and even the agony of mind dropped away like a discarded cloak.

She found several people, including the island's qualified nurse, inside the Clinic, and the three injured men were lying on camp beds. First Aid had been given them, and each of them was bandaged. The nurse turned to Diana with relief showing on her dusky face, and the other people moved away.

'I'm so glad you're here, Doctor. Would you take a look at this one first? He is more seriously injured than the other two.'

Diana moved to the nearest bed. The man

upon it was unconscious, one leg roughly splinted and bandaged, and there was a bandage around his head. Blood was seeping through the bandage on his leg, and Diana shook her head as she made a cursory examination. The leg was broken in two places, and someone was going to have a ticklish job repairing it. But the head injury concerned her more when she lifted the pad upon it. There was a slight depression in the dark skull and she knew without probing that the man had suffered a fracture. She looked up at the nurse.

'Have you requested the helicopter?' she demanded.

'Yes, Doctor. It will be sent as soon as it is free.'

Diana checked the other two men, and saw that they were less seriously injured, although one man had a broken left arm and the other's face was badly lacerated. She began working on them, attending the injuries and making them comfortable. It took her an hour to do all that she could, and she became worried about the most seriously injured of the trio. His eyes showed that damage had occurred inside his skull, and his pulse rate was dropping slowly. Shock was evident, and she did what she could to combat it, but as time went by she knew they would lose the man if he could not be quickly transported to hospital.

The nurse telephoned the hospital at St Flavia again, and learned that the helicopter would not be free for quite some time. Diana called in Jerry when she learned the news, and her face was grave as she outlined their problem. But Jerry shook his head when she finished.

'It isn't possible to fit a stretcher anywhere on the plane,' he said. 'She just isn't made to accommodate it. If he could sit up I'd risk him in the cockpit with me, but you say he's got to be kept as still as possible. Well you've ridden in the cockpit enough times to weigh up the situation for yourself. Would a ride like that kill him?'

'I think it would,' Diana said slowly, shaking her head. 'I wish now that you had a helicopter, Jerry!'

'They've talked about that for years,' he replied. 'But until the seaplane wears out there's little chance of getting another machine. Money is tight, as you know. They find it hard to get the vital equipment they need.'

'I know, but an incident like this makes the problem more acute. Nurse, will you try the hospital again? Tell them it is a matter of life and death.'

The nurse nodded and hurried to the telephone, and Diana paced the long room, her feet echoing in the silence. Outside the windows the darkness pressed against the panes as if interested in what was happening, and the stars pierced the velvet sky like chips of dry ice. Diana paused at a window and stared out into the shadows. Someone had lit a large bonfire on some waste ground, and she could see figures dancing around it. But the fire was too far away for her to hear the noise of the steel band. Life was going on the same for some people, she thought, and her tired mind cast back for a moment to her own troubles. She wondered if Fenton had sailed from St Flavia yet! Where would he go? Would he return to St Lydia, to the plantation there? Her heart ached as she considered, and then the nurse was returning and she forced her mind to concentrate upon the problems facing her.

'The helicopter has just left St Flavia,' the nurse reported. 'It will be here in forty-five minutes.'

Diana heaved a sigh and went to check the patients again. The policeman was sitting by the camp bed on which lay the least seriously wounded of the three men, and he was taking a statement, writing slowly in his notebook as the man gasped out the details of the incident.

Diana left the Clinic then, feeling the need for some fresh air. She stood in the darkness by the door, staring at the distant bonfire, hearing faintly the throbbing music that filtered through the night. The leaves were rustling on the nearby trees, as if disturbed by the music, and the faint breeze that touched Diana's face was cool and pleasant, scented by the many wild flowers growing around the Clinic. She took a deep breath and exhaled sharply.

Her mind seemed to belong to a stranger. Gone were all the familiar thoughts that made up her personality. There were gaps in her processing that would not refill by themselves. She seemed a stranger unto herself, like some female Rip Van Winkle in the moments of awakening after the marathon sleep. She was bewildered by what had taken place back there on St Flavia, and for a few moments she wished heartily that she did not have to return there. She had given her life to the service of others, and she felt that the least her patients could do was wish a little happiness upon her in the short time she had to herself.

Jerry Todd came out of the Clinic and lit a cigarette. He stood silently at Diana's side, and she heard his heavy breathing as he relaxed.

'You've got something on your mind,

Doctor,' he said shortly. 'Is there anything I can help with?'

'No, Jerry, thanks. It's nothing much, anyway.'

'It's Fenton Leigh, isn't it?' he pursued. 'I don't blame you, worrying about him. He was talking about leaving the island again, but the Inspector has told him to stick around for a few days longer.'

'He did?' Diana shook herself from her apathy. 'Are you sure, Jerry?'

'Of course I'm sure!' He glanced at her, his features indistinct in the shadows. 'Fenton is still under suspicion, I suppose.'

'They haven't found Jane Rutherford yet?' Diana shook her head as she wondered what had become of the girl.

'Not yet! I have a feeling that they won't find her alive when they do come upon her.'

'Surely not that!' Diana cringed a little as she recalled that Geoffrey Foster was involved with Jane Rutherford, or supposed to be. She caught her breath as she considered that Geoffrey was probably more involved than any could suspect. But Inspector Pollard knew all about Geoffrey, and she supposed that the policeman knew what he was doing.

The nurse emerged from the Clinic, and Diana turned to the girl, fearing the worst.

She did not hold out much hope for their patient's life. His condition had deteriorated since her arrival, and the galling thing was that she could do nothing for him. He needed surgical attention, and she had neither the place nor the equipment to attempt anything.

'I'm afraid the helicopter will be too late for us,' the nurse said, her dusky face glistening with sweat under the small yellow lamp that gleamed above the door of the Clinic.

'The patient?' Diana demanded, turning around and moving forward.

'I think he's dying.'

Diana shook her head and entered the Clinic, moving quickly to the side of the badly injured man. The policeman had finished his questioning of the other two men, and was standing in a corner drinking coffee from a battered enamel mug. He watched Diana intently as she sat down at the injured man's bedside. She took the pulse rate and lifted an eyelid, and shook her head. The man was sinking into a deep coma, and she didn't think he would come out of it. She had injected him to the limit, and there was nothing else she could do but wait.

The time seemed to loiter as they waited, but there was little change in the condition of the badly injured patient when Diana heard the first insistent note of an approaching helicopter. She went to the door of the building and saw that lights had been switched on to show the small landing place, and flickering red and green lights marked the position of the hovering machine. It came down slowly and made a perfect landing, and the crew jumped out with stretchers.

In a matter of moments the patients were loaded into the machine, and Diana gave instructions to the medical attendant aboard. Then they stepped back and the helicopter lifted gently from the ground and whirled quickly away, blotting out the stars as it swung and found its direction. When it had gone Diana heaved a long sigh of relief and looked around for Jerry. They were free to go home.

On the homeward trip she found her mind reverting to the problems she had pushed aside during the emergency. But she was tired now as they flew through the soft darkness. Her eyelids were heavy and her mind seemed sluggish. She could feel no real pain at the knowledge that Fenton was going away. But her breath seemed to stick in her throat when she considered what life would be like without him!

Despite the control she clamped upon her feelings she was tense as they swung down to land in the bay at St Flavia. Jerry had made such landings many times in his experience as a pilot for the doctor and they touched down softly and sped in to the shore. Diana was weary as she got out of the plane, and Jerry handed her bag to her, still cheerful despite the long day they had put in.

'See you in the morning, Doctor,' he said. 'But it's hardly worthwhile going to bed, is it?'

'We'd better get a few hours in, Jerry.' She smiled tiredly, her eyes flickering to the spot in the bay where Fenton had moored his schooner. She could see no lights, and a wistfulness seized hold of her. 'Goodnight.' The word trembled on her lips.

She walked to her car, and her mind went back to the moment when she had arrived so recklessly, with Geoff Foster close behind. She had imagined that her love for Fenton was so strong she didn't have to make a decision about him and her work, but as soon as she learned of the accident on Tara she had forgotten Fenton and sped off across the sea to do what she could. Her shoulders slumped a little as she got into her car. Fenton had spoken the truth when he said medicine was a way of life. She couldn't give it up that easily, and it seemed that she would have to if she insisted upon associating with the man she loved.

Her speed was slow on her way home, and she was deathly tired when she finally reached the house. She parked well away from the house, fearful that she would awaken her parents, and she felt in no mood to talk with her mother again. The moon was softly illuminating the island as she walked through the dust of the yard to the black pile of the house, and her eyes flickered towards Geoff's bungalow. There was still a light in his study. But he often worked late, or sat reading. She didn't want to see him again tonight, and she hurried into the house and quickly made her way to bed.

Before she slept she had to comfort her mind, and that seemed an impossible task. She could not help wondering where Fenton was at that time, and her thoughts stayed with him as she slowly sank down into slumber. She slept uneasily, but did not regain full consciousness until her accustomed time in the morning. When she did awaken she found her mind heavy with anticipation, and there was a dead spot inside her which encompassed all those hurtful thoughts of Fenton . . .

CHAPTER TEN

Mrs Brett was up when Diana went down the stairs, and there was a determined expression upon the woman's face as she met Diana in the hall.

'You're up early, Mother!' Diana had decided to act as if nothing had happened. She would go about her duties and keep herself busy in the hope that she would not have time to think of personal things.

'I wanted to talk to you, Diana!'

'Surely there's nothing more to say! You've accomplished what you set out to do last evening. Fenton is leaving and I shan't be seeing him again. The least you can do now is let me have some privacy for my feelings.'

'I'm sorry, dear. I acted for your own good, and Fenton Leigh agreed with me when I pointed out the situation to him. I'll give him that much! He was very nice about it and he decided that I was right. If he thinks I'm right then I must be, and I know I must help you where I can.'

'So it's all over and done with,' Diana smiled thinly. 'You can telephone Doctor Hamilton this morning and tell him my brief fling is over, that I'm back to normal, suitably cowed by the knowledge that I almost lost my job!'

'Don't sound so bitter, Diana! I was only thinking of your best interests.'

'That's the stock excuse used by most people when they want to interfere in someone's life.' Diana smiled as she walked around her mother and entered the kitchen. She went through the routine of preparing breakfast although she wasn't in the least bit interested in eating. Mrs Brett stood in the doorway, watching her, worried now, wondering how best to get around the situation she had created. Diana looked at her mother as she sat down at the table.

'Don't look so worried, Mother,' she said lightly. 'You should be very happy that you've saved your daughter from a male monster. That's what Fenton is! You've saved me from a great deal of trouble. Now my job is still secure and I have nothing to worry about. You have done me a great service, Mother.'

'Perhaps you don't think so right now, dear, but in a few days, when you've had time to think it over, I'm sure you'll agree that I acted with your interests at heart. Where are you going today?' It was a clumsy attempt to change the subject, and Diana smiled.

'I don't know yet. I haven't called the hospital.'

'You were in very late! What happened? Was it a bad case?'

Diana ate some of her breakfast as she recounted the incidents of the previous night. But only half her mind was upon what she was saying. She couldn't help wondering about Fenton. He had gone back to St Lydia? Would he stay there? Was there a chance that she would see him again? Could his love be strong enough to bring him after her? She felt like dropping everything and hurrying to his side! But there seemed little hope of another meeting. He had been decisive when he spoke, and she knew she could not give up her work. They could not stop her practising, but if they sacked her from this position she wouldn't be able to get another job anywhere in the islands. She would have to go far away, and try to start again, and that would mean not seeing Fenton anyway. She knew she was beaten, and the knowledge was bitter and hard inside her.

When she left the house to go to the hospital for her daily orders she saw Geoffrey standing on his verandah, and he called to her as she started towards her car. Diana suppressed a sigh and waited for him, and he came across quickly, his feet scuffing up the dust in the early morning sunshine. His face was showing tension, and she wondered if Inspector Pollard had seen him yet about his association with the missing Jane Rutherford. Thinking of that, she could not help wondering how he could love her and yet see another girl secretly. She supposed that her trouble in seeing Fenton arose from the fact that Jane Rutherford was missing and Fenton might have had something to do with the girl's disappearance. But Geoffrey might know something about that!

'Diana, I waited up last night until you got in,' he said, watching her face closely in an attempt to divine her frame of mind. 'Didn't you see my light?'

'I did. But surely you didn't expect me to come and see you!'

'We could have had a talk.'

'There's nothing we can talk about! You must feel proud of yourself, talking to my mother behind my back about Fenton and me.'

'I was only thinking of you!'

'That's what they all say! But you acted out of jealousy, Geoff. I don't understand you! You told me you loved me! But you've been seeing Jane Rutherford on the side.'

His face showed his shock, and he almost gasped as her words sank home. Diana set her teeth into her bottom lip, and she could have kicked herself for saying it. But surely Inspector Pollard had spoken to Geoff about Jane Rutherford.

'So you're the one who told the Inspector about me and Jane!' His brown eyes glittered in the sunlight as he stared at her. 'How did you know about it?'

'A lot of people know about it, and there's talk that Jane was in an interesting condition. Is that why she's disappeared, Geoff?'

'That's none of your damned business!' He spoke roughly, and turned abruptly and strode away from her, his face showing embarrassment.

Diana watched him go, her mind needle sharp. She knew guilt when she saw it. So Geoffrey had been having an affair with the missing girl! And he had professed love for her! She compressed her lips as she watched him hurry back to his bungalow. How could one tell when a man was serious or not? Had Fenton merely been amusing himself at her expense? He had found it easy, apparently, to go away and leave her! She shook her head and went on to her car, and she drove steadily into town. But before she reached Tenka a car swept past her at reckless speed, and she saw with mounting surprise that it was Geoffrey's. He seemed to leave her standing, and she increased speed a little, but she saw only his dust all the way to town, and when she arrived there was no sign of him or his car.

Going into the hospital, Diana reported for duty and picked up her schedules for the day. She found she had to fly to St Guill first, then on to Tope, where she had first met Fenton. It seemed so long ago now, she reflected as she checked the lists. She had to go on to Rango if there was time later, but it wasn't important. She made up her mind to go to Rango. She wanted to work as hard as possible. She had to keep her mind occupied every waking minute.

'How are those three men we brought in from Tara last night?' she asked the clerk in the office.

'One of them died shortly after admission,' she was told, and she nodded. There had been little hope for him at the outset. 'The other two are making progress. But before you leave, Doctor, would you go along to Doctor Hamilton's office? He wants to see you before you depart.'

'At this time of the morning?' Diana was surprised. 'He doesn't usually come into the hospital until I'm well on my way!'

'He's early today, and especially wants to see you.'

Diana nodded and left her bag in the office while she visited her superior. A trickle of anticipation ran through her as she tapped at his door, and her heart seemed to lurch when his steady voice bade her enter. She took a deep breath and steeled herself, then entered the office.

Doctor Hamilton was a tall, heavily built man in his early fifties, and his wrinkled face showed the nature of his calling. Blue eyes were gentle and compassionate, and his shock of wiry hair was clipped short so that it stood up like new corn.

'Diana!' He got to his feet and moved around the desk to pull out a chair for her, and Diana went forward and sat down.

'Good morning, Doctor,' she said formally, and he studied her intent face as he went back to his seat.

'I wanted to talk to you before you left this morning because I felt that any delay might add to your feelings on this delicate subject that has come up.'

Diana blinked, but said nothing. She had guessed that Fenton would be the subject of discussion. But the way people went on about the man she loved, one would think he was the Devil himself!

'It's really none of my business,' Doctor Hamilton said evenly. 'You can tell me to mind my own business if you wish, Diana, but before you do I would like to point out a few facts to you.'

'Before you go any further, Doctor, perhaps I ought to tell you that Fenton Leigh plans to leave the islands very shortly and never return.'

'Oh!' Hamilton took a deep breath and then exhaled sharply. 'I see!' He nodded slowly. 'I took the liberty of calling your mother yesterday to learn what facts I could. I had several calls from your nearer patients, and they all followed the same line. I had to do something. I am responsible for much that you do. All these complaints were about your association with Mr Leigh.'

'There is such a thing as defamation of character, Doctor. I know of nothing that Fenton has done that is against the law! What did these well-wishers have to say about this association of mine?'

'They didn't think it right that a person in such a responsible position should associate with a man who is an ex-doctor. If you had been following any profession but medicine then it wouldn't have mattered, but Leigh is an ex-doctor, and it's only natural that people are afraid you might adopt some of his attitudes. He was found guilty of unprofessional conduct, remember, so the question of defamation of character doesn't enter into it.'

'Well, that is all beside the point,' Diana got to her feet. She stared down into his lined face for a moment. 'Fenton is going away and I shall be carrying out my duties as usual. Perhaps you would inform those patients who complained, Doctor, and set their tiny minds at rest.' She paused and her blue eyes glinted. 'I expect I could name those patients who complained, couldn't I? The first would be Alice Reid, and the others would be Mrs Reid's close circle of gossip-mongers!'

'I don't blame you for feeling strongly about this, Diana. I feel most uneasy myself. But you are a doctor and must maintain an irreproachable attitude and character. The fact that patients have complained is enough for me to consider taking action. That is why I called your mother. I know what you feel about medicine, Diana, and if trouble came from this association you would regret it for the rest of your life.'

'Of course, Doctor. But, as I said, the situation has changed without too much trouble and everything is as it was before. If there is nothing else then I'd better be on my way. I have a lot of travelling to do today.'

'Certainly.' Hamilton got to his feet and came around the desk, and he put an arm around Diana's shoulders as he walked her to the door. 'I'm so sorry you've been caused this anxiety. I know how you must be feeling. I only wish I could tell you to make what plans you wish for the future.'

'My future is all mapped out for me, Doctor,' Diana said as she departed. 'I shall be attending the patients in these islands until I'm too old to climb into the seaplane.'

'You won't be using that seaplane much longer.'

'No?' Diana frowned as she stared at him.

'After last night's incidents I feel justified in having your present mode of transport changed. Perhaps the life of that accident victim might have been saved if you could have flown him back here without that long delay.'

'I've been saying that all along,' Diana pointed out.

'Well we'll see what can be done.'

'Will Jerry Todd still be my pilot?'

'I expect so. He knows as much about your routine as you do. I have sounded him out about this, and although he will be disappointed at losing the seaplane, he understands that it is for the best, and he's looking forward to taking lessons in flying a helicopter.' Hamilton patted Diana's shoulder, and she smiled as she turned away. Fenton seemed even farther away from her as she prepared to start her day's duties. 'Good luck with today's flying,' Hamilton called after her, and she turned and lifted a hand to him.

The day seemed longer than usual, and Diana had to keep making an effort to maintain her usual alertness about her work. They landed at St Guill and pressure of work kept her busy until early afternoon. She was tired by the time they were ready to take off for Tope, and Diana knew she had not been successful in keeping her mood secret. She had hardly spoken to Jerry during the first flight, and she sensed that he was itching to discuss what lay closest to her heart.

It wasn't until they were in the air and flying towards Tope that Jerry spoke about Fenton, and as the name was mentioned Diana wished she could close her ears, but what Jerry had to say made her straighten in her seat.

'Did you hear that Fenton Leigh was ordered not to sail from St Flavia?'

'No!' Diana caught her breath. 'What's happened? Why didn't you tell me before?'

'You didn't seem to be in a very good mood this morning!' Jerry grinned at her. 'I guessed you'd had trouble with Fenton. But there's a policeman aboard his schooner to make sure he doesn't sail. So Inspector Pollard isn't completely satisfied that he isn't involved in the girl's disappearance.'

'Hasn't anyone seen the girl yet?'

'No. She's probably got away from the island all right, but how?'

'That's the big question. But where is Fenton anchored? I didn't see his lights last night, and the schooner wasn't in the bay this morning.'

'I saw you looking for it.' Jerry grinned tightly as he glanced at her. 'The Inspector made Fenton sail around to that cove where he was the other night. Your place is back of the ridge overlooking it.'

Diana knew only too well where the spot was, and she relived that wonderful evening when she had swum out to the ship. Her heart seemed to constrict with misery, and she blinked her eyes sharply against the tears that rose unbidden. How could she forget Fenton when he seemed to be up to his neck in trouble? Surely this was the time when he needed someone to stand by him! What must he be thinking about this mess into which he had sailed? How could people be so cruel as to blame him for everything that happened when he was around? But she knew the answer to that without having to think too deeply. He had been a doctor when he fell from grace, and a doctor ought to have been above the frailties affecting every other human. She knew it was the same in her case, and the knowledge didn't help to ease the tension or the pain she was feeling.

Tope came into sight, and there was a queer tugging sensation around Diana's heart as they swooped down to land on the smooth blue waters. The last time they had come here she had met Fenton! It had been a turning point in her life. For years she had gone blithely on her way, immensely happy with her life, certain that she lacked nothing! Then Fenton came across her path and she had known in an instant that her former life had been incomplete. She was too aware of what she had been missing, and although her glimpse of paradise had been brief, it had also been vivid, and she could not accept that she had to go without the man she loved in order to continue her way of life.

A restlessness seized hold of her as she left the seaplane. She attended her patients and made the island round as always, and there was nothing in her face or her manner to divulge her sorrow. Everything was as always, except the cold knowledge in her breast which would not permit her peace. She returned to the seaplane and found Jerry waiting for her. It was at this point on their previous visit when the schooner had showed, and her heart seemed heavy as she scanned the bay in the vain hope of finding history repeating itself.

But Fenton was practically under arrest at St Flavia! She considered that as she waited for Jerry to take off. He gained the cockpit at her side and looked at her before switching on.

'Do we go on to Rango or back to St Flavia?' he demanded.

'We'd better go to Rango! It will mean getting back to St Flavia a lot later this evening, but if we leave it until tomorrow, when we have to visit Sama, we'll have too much to do in one day.'

'You're the boss. Hold tight.' He grinned at her and started the engine, and Diana sighed with a shudder as she settled herself down again.

Her mind kept its hold upon the thoughts about Fenton, and as they went on, flying farther away from St Flavia, she was keenly aware that time and distance was an insurmountable barrier between her and the man she loved. But a growing decision in her mind was slowly coming to a climax.

She would have to see Fenton again, if only to find out what was happening to him. She had to go to him.

They reached Rango and landed in a lagoon two miles from the sea. There was a collection of nondescript little buildings around the lagoon, and a crowd of natives were already gathered at the landing stage. Diana lost some of the frost invading her mind when she heard their carefree chattering as she climbed out of the cockpit, and she forced away her thoughts and waved cheerfully as she went to greet them.

She checked five patients and inoculated several children. But there were no serious cases for her to deal with. Jerry checked over his beloved engine while he waited for her, and when she was through Diana was filled with leaping relief. Now they could go back to St Flavia, and the first thing she would do when she got off duty was visit Fenton!

The decision lightened her considerably, and when Jerry took the plane up to five hundred feet her spirits seemed to rise accordingly. They were heading for home! She sighed sharply and tried to contain her impatience. The brightness of the long hours of sunshine had given her a slight headache, and she felt dazzled by the reflection of the sun from the smooth waters far below.

They flew the thirty-odd miles back to Tope, and passed over the island on their way to St Flavia, travelling westward at one hundred and twenty miles an hour. Dusk was closing in along the horizon by the time they sighted the larger island, and Diana tried to control her mounting excitement as they went down in a flat dive to land.

St Flavia looked pretty from the air when the town lights were on, and the bay was ringed by twinkling pools of brilliance. Away from the town, in the indistinct darkness of the interior of the island, tiny clusters of lights marked the nearer small villages, and solitary lights showed where the most remote habitations were situated. Diana was always thrilled by the sight, and this evening proved no exception, despite her great anticipation. Spray flew as the floats kissed the surface of the bay, and Jerry throttled down as they made a perfect landing. They headed in to the quay and Jerry climbed out to make fast. Diana felt strangely elated as she stepped on to firm ground, and she took her bag from Jerry and thanked him for his labours of the day.

'See you in the morning, Doctor,' he retorted cheerfully. 'I hope you'll have a nice evening off duty.'

'There won't be much of the evening left when I get through and can call it a day,' she replied, smiling faintly. She hurried away to her car and drove swiftly through the town, hoping against hope that Fenton's ship was still in the cove. She reached home, but did not enter the house. She left the car out of sight and earshot of the house and locked it, then hurried along the path that led over the ridge. She could wait no longer to see if Fenton was still around.

Her heart seemed to miss a beat when she topped the ridge and saw the lights of the schooner below her. Breathing heavily in relief, she watched for a moment, recalling that evening when she had swum out to the ship. Impulses were flashing through her, and she knew she was not strong enough to fight them off. She would swim out to the ship again, and make Fenton see her. If only she could talk with him for a few moments it would help her get rid of the dead feeling deep inside.

She turned with lighter steps and went back along the path. Getting into her car again, she drove up to the house and parked as if she had just arrived. She took her bag into the house, hoping against hope that her parents had gone out for the evening. She felt that she could not take another lecture, and she didn't want anyone to know where she was going.

Her mother was in the hall when Diana entered the house, and Diana suppressed her disappointment and showed a casual expression as she closed the door.

'Hello, Mother! No surprises for me this evening, I hope!'

'No, Diana. How did you make out today?'

'I've been busy.'

'What are your plans for this evening?'

Diana glanced at her watch. 'The evening is almost over,' she retorted. 'There's nothing you want me to do, is there?' Her voice was steady, even, and there was nothing in her tones to suggest that what had taken place the previous evening had upset her. She could see relief growing in her mother's face, and knew the episode would soon be forgotten, but she had no intention of forgetting it herself!

'There's nothing I want you to do, but Geoffrey has had a talk with me, and I'd like you to spare me a little time when you've rested from your day's work.'

'Geoffrey!' Something in Diana's tone gave her mother a start of surprise, and Diana saw trouble ahead as her instincts gave her the warning signs. 'What's wrong with Geoffrey?'

'He saw Jane Rutherford after Fenton Leigh did.'

'What?' Diana could not control her surprise. 'Tell me about it, Mother!'

'Jane was last seen early in the afternoon, when she was down on the quay.'

'That was when Fenton saw her!' Diana narrowed her eyes. 'When did Geoffrey see her?'

'That same evening. He went along to his motor cruiser to check it over and found Jane aboard, waiting for him.'

'Has he told the police?' Diana could not prevent a tremor running through her voice.

'He didn't think anything of it then. Jane wasn't posted as missing until later.'

'What did he do about her?' Diana was too eager to await her mother's account.

'He saw her ashore, and told her to go home. She tried to get him to take her to Sama, where she could catch a boat to Trinidad. But it's a round trip of a hundred and thirty miles, and Geoffrey wouldn't attempt it.'

'So what happened to Jane?'

'She went ashore and hasn't been seen since.'

'Why hasn't Geoffrey gone to Inspector Pollard with this tale? He knows that a search is being made for the girl. He's heard how people think Fenton had something to do with Jane's disappearance.'

'He's afraid of being coupled with the girl. You see, she told him that she's in trouble.'

'In trouble?' Diana stared into her mother's face. She let her mind consider what she had heard. 'Why should she go to Geoff?' she demanded. 'Surely she would go to the man responsible.'

'You don't think Geoff had anything to do with her, do you?'

'You sound surprised at the idea.' Diana shook her head. 'Yet you were quite ready to believe the worst about Fenton. But I have heard that Geoffrey was with Jane on several occasions, and once they were overheard to be arguing. What did you advise Geoffrey to do, Mother?'

'I told him he ought to see Inspector Pollard at once.'

'And has he?'

'I don't know. I don't think so. He's not worried about having to clear his name, or anything like that. He just doesn't want any talk about himself.'

'But he was quite prepared to help along the scandal about Fenton.' Diana breathed deeply. 'I'm going to ring Inspector Pollard myself and acquaint him with this new evidence. It might help him pinpoint Jane's movements.'

'I wouldn't do that if I were you!' Mrs Brett sounded alarmed. 'Geoffrey told me in the strictest confidence, but I just had to tell you.'

'Something has to be done to break this deadlock that seems to have us all in its power,' Diana said firmly. 'Mother, you should know better than to meddle in a business like this. If Geoffrey does have anything to answer for then the sooner he does so the better. I'm going to ring the Inspector, and right now.'

CHAPTER ELEVEN

Diana put a call through to the police station, but learned that Inspector Pollard was not in. She arranged to call again later, and went to her room to prepare for her visit to Fenton. She put on her swimsuit under her clothes and didn't take a towel with her, not wanting anyone in the house to know where she was going. She sneaked downstairs and went through the kitchen, warning Vinia Owen not to tell anyone about her movements. When she stepped out into the shadows surrounding the house the cool night air touched her face, and she took a long breath and released it slowly. There was tension inside her that could not be moved, and she set off along the path with slow steps, hardly daring to carry out her plan, but afraid that she might lose any slim chance she had of seeing Fenton again.

The information she had about Geoffrey seemed to convince her that he knew more about Jane Rutherford than anyone guessed, and she wanted to tell Fenton. If there was a policeman aboard Fenton's ship then Inspector Pollard must be fairly certain that Fenton could do much more to help the enquiries along, but this new information changed matters completely, to Diana's way of thinking.

The path was dark, but she knew each yard of the way, and she was breathless when she reached the top of the ridge. She peered eagerly for the ship, and was reassured when she saw its lights in the cove. She went down the slope to the beach with a rush, and walked through the trees to the sand, her heart pumping madly as she prepared to see Fenton again. The past twenty-four hours had been a misery of existence, and she never wanted to face another time like it.

She undressed slowly in the shadows, and put her clothes under a tree, standing for a moment with the breeze caressing her skin. She looked around before venturing to the water's edge and, satisfied that it was all clear, she slipped into the water with hardly a splash and struck out for the ship.

This time she wouldn't let the Polynesian scare her! She smiled inwardly as she recalled her panic of the previous trip. But she kept a strict watch on the surrounding water as she neared the silent ship. The lights that showed seemed to beckon her on, and her mind was flooded with emotion as she trod water under the bows of the vessel.

This time Zero did not appear in the water at her side, and she reached up out of the water and took hold of the stern of the dinghy moored alongside. She pulled herself into the boat and then swung upon the deck of the ship. A dark figure came silently towards her as she straightened and looked around, and the next instant a strong hand had seized her arm. She recognized Zero, and he muttered something unintelligible as he pushed her towards the companionway. He held her tightly as if fearing she might slip away from him, and he called urgently below. A moment later Fenton appeared in the companionway, and Diana was disappointed that the night was so dark, because she could not read his expression.

'You'd better come below,' he said slowly, and there was no surprise in his tones. 'As a matter of fact I've been expecting you.'

She warmed to his words, and hoped that he had already thought twice about his decision to go away. She followed him down to his cabin, and he threw a towel at her while she stood dripping water over the bottom step of the ladder. Their eyes met and held the gaze that passed between them, and Diana fancied that he was a very worried man.

'Fenton,' she began, and stopped, not knowing what to add.

'Diana, I want to apologize for what I said last night. I went back to your home a little later, but you had already gone out on that emergency flight.'

'You went back?' she demanded. 'Why?'

'To tell you that I love you too much to consider going away!' His eyes seemed filled with inner fires as he stared at her. 'I know it is wrong, but this thing is stronger than I am. It will be up to you to send me away if you feel that I would menace your career. I can't find the necessary strength myself. I'm a fool, Diana, but I love you!'

'Fenton!' She dropped the towel and ran to him, hurtling herself into his arms, and she was heedless of the fact that she was dressed only in a wet swimsuit.

He gathered her gently into his arms and held her close, his shirt wet from her, and he stared hungrily into her face, his lean features showing so much relief that Diana felt like crying for joy.

'Diana, this day has been like a horrible nightmare. I've been restless and confused. There was a policeman aboard all day to prevent me sailing.'

'Isn't he still here?' she demanded.

'No. They took him off. I'm free to leave now.'

'Why? What's happened to make the Inspector relent?'

'I don't know! They never tell you anything. But I suppose they don't have enough evidence against me.'

'You weren't the last man to see Jane Rutherford on the island,' she said joyfully, and hurried to explain what her mother had told her. His face changed expression a little as he listened, and when she fell silent he thrust out his underlip and stared thoughtfully into space.

'What's on your mind, darling?' she demanded.

'Quite a number of things, sweetheart. But dry yourself, and I'll give you a robe to put on. This sort of thing isn't doing your reputation any good.'

'I learned that from my first visit.' She smiled slowly. 'But I have the feeling it doesn't matter so much this time. You're not under suspicion of having done something dreadful to Jane Rutherford.'

'Well, that's a relief, anyway.' He smiled in his turn, then held her close and kissed her fervently.

Diana closed her eyes and let herself slip slowly away from reality. If she needed any further proof that Fenton was the only man for her then that close contact between them provided all the evidence. She thrilled to him, responding to his passion with surprising strength, and she could feel all her new decisions falling apart under the strain. Life was so short that one had to take happiness wherever it lay. This man, a near complete stranger, was all she wanted in this world. If they wouldn't let her career continue because of him then she would throw her career overboard. A woman had to make sacrifices for love. That was the order of things, and had always been so. Why should she expect life to be any different for her?

'Fenton!' She looked up into his face. 'I love you so much. I said as much yesterday, but it needed this parting to bring home the truth in no uncertain manner. Today has been dreadful for me, thinking that I would never see you again. I never want to face another like it!'

'You won't, dearest!' His voice was husky with unaccustomed emotion. 'Don't you worry about a thing. I'm not going to lose sight of you. We'll never have to part.'

'But what about this business of Jane Rutherford? It affects us all, and until she is found no one will ever believe that you had nothing to do with her disappearance.'

'I've got a good mind to talk to Geoffrey Foster myself,' Fenton said. His face was grim as he spoke. 'He doesn't like me because of you, and I'm sure he had something to do with the stories going around the island about us!'

'I received a warning from Doctor Hamilton this morning.' Diana suppressed a sigh. 'Geoffrey was the only one who knew I swam out here the night before last.' She shook her head slowly. 'But it wouldn't help if you interfered now, Fenton. Let Inspector Pollard handle this matter. I'm going to ring him when I get back to the house, and tell him what I know about Geoffrey. He can sort it out better than we can.'

Fenton nodded slowly. 'I'll be happy to get this settled,' he said. 'Is there any chance that you can get some time off from this eternal flying around the islands? You don't work non-stop through the year, do you?'

'I have a holiday due me, but I don't feel like asking for it just yet.'

'I'd like to get you right away from the islands.' His voice was brittle. 'I don't know what you must think of me in the light of all the gossip that's going round. But I promise, Diana, that you'll never have cause to regret the day you met me.'

'I'm sure I won't.' She turned away and took up the towel which she had dropped, and as she wrapped it around herself she felt as if all her troubles had been collected together, locked in a lead-lined box, and dumped overboard. She was so elated that she knew she could face any disaster so long as Fenton was there at her side. She could not doubt the feelings inside her. This was true love and no one had any right to prohibit it. She went to him again and thrust herself into his embrace. 'Fenton, I know this will work out. I can feel it in my bones.'

'Well your optimism does you proud!' He smiled down at her, his arms strong about her slim body. 'I'm sure nothing can go wrong for a girl who is as good and wonderful as you. But we'd better not sit down and just hope that something will turn up for us, that some good fairy will wave her wand and make all our troubles disappear. It doesn't happen like that in reality. We have to do something about the situation if we want it to work out.'

'What do you suggest?' Her blue eyes were bright as she watched him.

'I'll row you ashore and you can make that telephone call to the Inspector. I'd like to see his face when he gets the news! He was almost certain at one time that I was the last man to see Jane Rutherford, and that I knew what happened to her after she disappeared.'

'Let's go,' Diana said instantly. 'You'll come to the house with me, Fenton?'

'Won't you want to keep this secret for a few days at least?' His eyes were steady, filled with love as he watched her. 'Your career is still important to you.'

'Not as important as you.' She sighed heavily, filled with so many uplifting emotions that she was hard put to contain them all. 'Let's go make that telephone call. I have a feeling that it will be one of the most important in our lives.'

'Geoff Foster certainly has got a lot of explaining to do!' Fenton shook his head slowly. 'But the truth will out eventually, Diana. That was why I changed my mind about leaving you. I knew the truth would come out, and all I had to do was wait for the right moment.'

They went up on deck and Fenton gave

orders to Zero, who stood like a black shadow on the deck. The Polynesian spoke rapidly in his own tongue, and Diana waited while Fenton replied. As they were getting into the dinghy, Diana asked Fenton what the native had said.

'He saw a swimmer in the water some time ago, but didn't go in after him because there was no immediate danger to the ship.'

'Was it a man?' Diana asked.

'Zero thought so, but I warned him the police might still be taking a close interest in the ship, and it might have been a policeman on water duty.' His tones were light-hearted, and Diana smiled despite the sudden tension that filtered into her.

Fenton rowed ashore, and Diana went to the spot where she had left her clothes. She donned them quickly and slipped her feet into her sandals. Fenton took her arm as they climbed the slope to the top of the ridge, and when they paused on the top to regain their breath Diana slipped into his arms.

The island was silent and still under the soft moonlight, and the stretch of sea beyond the cove seemed like a silver land of enchantment as it glittered right to the distant horizon. It looked solid enough to stand on, and Diana caught her breath as the beauty of the shadowed scene caught her imagination.

Fenton's arms were strong about her. That fact alone was sufficient to send her into ecstatic conjecture. She looked up into his dark face, and he bent and kissed her demandingly. She felt a surge of emotion start through her, and knew no other man could ever move her like this. She had found her soul-mate, and nothing and no one was going to separate them ever again.

They walked in silence along the path back to the house, and Diana felt as if she were walking on air. This wonderful sensation proved to her that nothing else mattered. She would go on doing her duty if they would let her, but she would not blame herself if she could not. She had only one life and she wanted some happiness in it.

When they reached the house some of Diana's joy receded, and she paused at the front door and looked up into Fenton's face. He must have read her mind for he smiled, his teeth glinting briefly, and he stepped back a pace.

'I'll remain out of sight if you wish,' he suggested. 'I know there will be trouble if we're seen together.'

'Nonsense! I'm not ashamed of you, and I'm not going to have you skulking around in the shadows. If anyone objects to you being in my company then we'll learn about it to our faces.'

'I admire your courage.' Smiling, he came to her side, and she opened the door with a show of confidence she was far from feeling and led the way into the hall.

Mrs Brett showed herself in the doorway of the lounge and stared at them as if she could not believe her eyes. Diana reached for the telephone, glancing at Fenton, who remained by the door. Mrs Brett came into the hall and approached them as if Fenton were a mad dog on a flimsy leash. Diana watched her mother's face intently as she dialled the number she wanted.

'Don't bother to say anything, Mother,' she said suddenly. 'You'll only make a scene. There's nothing you can do about this situation.'

Mrs Brett sighed and nodded slowly. She stood watching Fenton as if she suspected he might suddenly run off with the silver, and Fenton watched Diana as she made her call.

'Inspector Pollard! I'm glad I've reached you. Yes, this is Doctor Brett! What's the latest on this situation regarding Jane Rutherford? Has the girl been found yet?'

'She's still missing, Doctor,' Pollard replied. 'But you'll be interested to know that I've lifted the restriction from Fenton

Leigh's movements. I'm almost certain now that he knows nothing of the girl. More than that I'm afraid I can't tell you. But if you are still worried about Leigh then you'll be more than relieved to know that my investigations practically clear him.'

'I have some information for you, Inspector.'

'Really?' Interest sharpened his tones, Diana noticed, and she told him what her mother had said about Geoffrey Foster's admission regarding Jane Rutherford. 'That's very interesting, Doctor! Foster's name keeps cropping up when I talk to people about Jane Rutherford. I have had a talk with him about the girl and he denied seeing her on the day she disappeared. Is he at the plantation now?'

'Just a moment, Inspector!' Diana covered the mouthpiece with an eager hand and looked up at her mother. 'Is Geoff around the place, Mother?'

'I haven't seen him. He went out in his car earlier and hasn't returned, I'm certain.'

Diana nodded. 'He's not here, Inspector!'

'Thank you, Doctor! I'll look into this matter, and if Foster does return there, don't mention any of this to him, will you?'

'Not a word!' Diana replaced the receiver and turned to face Fenton. 'Well that should take care of some of the loose ends lying around,' she declared.

'You shouldn't have done that, Diana.' There was a reproachful note in Mrs Brett's tones. 'Geoffrey told me that information in the strictest confidence.'

'It's your duty and mine to report anything significant to the police,' Diana retorted. 'Or would you rather keep quiet and have everyone suspecting an innocent man? Fenton is innocent, but he's been subjected to some humiliating treatment these past few days.'

'I'm sorry, Mr Leigh,' Mrs Brett said. 'But yesterday there was some doubt about you. I would be a poor mother indeed if I didn't care about my daughter, don't you agree?'

'I do, Mrs Brett.' Fenton smiled slowly. 'I'm glad you have been taking good care of her. But I can assure you that she will never regret the day she met me.'

'I hope other people will be as understanding,' Diana's mother said worriedly. 'Alice Reid was here a short time ago, and she's still filled with poison against you, Mr Leigh.'

'I've got used to that sort of thing!' He smiled as he met Diana's eyes. 'My only hope is that Diana will get used to it. She could get hurt by some of the things she might hear.'

'Well you'll always be welcome in this house.' Mrs Brett smiled at Diana.

'Thank you.' Fenton nodded slowly.

'Thank you, Mother!' Diana ran to her mother's side and put her arms around the older woman's neck. She kissed her mother impulsively. 'I knew you would come round!'

'You're not the kind of girl to make a mistake, Diana,' Mrs Brett said cheerfully. 'Your instincts have always guided you correctly. If you think Fenton is the right man for you then I'm bound to accept your decision without question. But we're going to have a hard time convincing some of the other people who count. Doctor Hamilton called me today and mentioned the talk he'd had with you. He's convinced you've come to your senses. But it isn't as easy as that. If we're to get other people to accept Fenton then I've got to show everyone that I accept him wholeheartedly.'

'I knew you'd come round to my way of thinking,' Diana said happily. 'I need you on my side, Mother.'

'I'm only concerned with your happiness and welfare,' Mrs Brett said hopefully.

'Then we're all on the same side,' Fenton said, winking at Diana.

Diana glanced at her watch. She was very tired, but her happiness overwhelmed any other emotion that tried to get through her mind, and she moved to Fenton's side.

'Let's go for a stroll,' she said. 'I shan't be able to sleep yet, and I need some exercise after being cooped up in the seaplane for long stretches at a time.'

'Gladly,' Fenton replied, opening the front door. He looked at Mrs Brett. 'Thank you for seeing Diana's point of view.'

Diana sighed heavily with relief as they stepped out into the moonlight, and Fenton took her arm and squeezed it lovingly. Now her happiness was complete, and she knew that no matter what happened she wouldn't worry while Fenton was around. He had changed her life completely, and now she wouldn't want to revert to the old, uneventful ways for anything in the world. He was her choice, and nothing would be permitted to stand in the way of their happiness!

They walked towards the road, then cut across the nearer fields to a babbling brook which was Diana's favourite spot. The night was close about them, friendly with its uncertain cover, and the leaves murmured on the trees and the scent of the wild flowers was wonderful in Diana's nostrils. She breathed deeply, and could feel a sense of magic creep into her mind. She clutched Fenton's arm in an attempt to grasp reality, and her senses were heightened, keener than usual.

'What a beautiful evening,' she said softly.

'This is just perfect, Fenton.'

'All our days together will be like this,' he responded slowly. His eyes were keen as he put his face close to hers and stared into her features. 'I love you, Diana! I love you more than life itself. I've looked for you ever since I've been old enough to have a picture of my dream woman in my mind. Little did I know you were here in the islands, and it took my father's death to bring me back to you.'

'Say it was Fate!' she said, with her eyes shining.

'Destiny is a better word. You're my destiny! Diana, you're the most beautiful girl in the world! I love you to distraction.'

She closed her eyes as he took her into his arms, and the sound of the rushing water formed a soothing background to their love. The wild scent of the climbing flowers about them sent strange sensations through Diana's mind and she found it difficult to believe this was really happening to her. This was dreamlike, but she was happy to know that it was reality! The future seemed assured! She was certain of that!

CHAPTER TWELVE

It was late when Diana finally found herself back on her doorstep, but she didn't look at her watch for fear of breaking the wonderful spell that held her. Fenton took her into his arms once again, and she thrilled to the whispered words of love that he spoke. But he finally drew away and held her at arm's length, his face shadowed, but his eyes bright in the gloom.

'Diana, you have to be out early in the morning,' he said softly. 'You must go in now.'

'I'm going, although I don't feel a bit sleepy now. No doubt I shall pay for it in the morning. But shall I see you tomorrow, Fenton?'

'You will, and every day! I don't know how I'm going to tear myself away and get back to St Lydia! I shall have to try and settle down and help with the work. Willard has been good about my return as it is, but I shall have to shoulder some of the responsibilities.'

'Wouldn't you want to go back into medicine?' she asked.

'I have thought about it, but there seems

little chance of that particular miracle occurring. We'll talk about the future at a later date, my dearest!'

He kissed her again and Diana turned reluctantly to open the door. She looked at him again. Her heart seemed to swell with emotion, and there was a trembling sensation inside which seemed to come from a bubble of love that was swelling and enlarging beyond all control.

'Shall I come out to the ship tomorrow evening?' she asked.

'I think perhaps I'd better row ashore for you. I'll come here for you, Diana.'

'Good!' She was pleased. 'I shall be waiting for you. I usually get through for the day around seven-thirty.'

'I'll be seeing you.' He leaned forward and kissed her lightly upon the mouth, then backed away. He lifted a hand to her and Diana clutched at it for a moment, loath to let him go, but he laughed gently and disengaged himself, then started away from the house, his feet making no noise in the yard.

Diana stood watching his departure until his figure faded among the trees along the path that led over the ridge. She sighed deeply, exalted far above her normal plane, and she didn't want to come down from that high peak. She wanted her wonderful feelings to live on and on.

She seemed to fall into a reverie as she stood at the door, and her thoughts retraced every step of the emotional way she had trod that evening. She was happier now than she had ever been, and something inside her seemed to say that she would never have any doubts or troubles again. Even the warning that Maria the nurse had given her was fading from her mind.

When she heard a faint noise across the yard she stiffened, thinking perhaps Fenton had returned, and she narrowed her eyes and tried to locate his figure, but there was no movement in that direction, and the sound came again, from the area around Geoff Foster's bungalow. She turned and stared into the shadows concealing the bungalow, and fancied that she saw movement. But it might have been her imagination! She frowned as she waited, but the sound was not repeated, and her thoughts shifted from Fenton to Geoffrey Foster.

Entering the house, she went quickly to bed, trying to force her mind to forget the situation that surrounded them. The fact that her mother was on their side now promised a great deal, and Diana was in a happy frame of mind as she sank into well earned slumber . . .

Next morning she was awake early, and as she went down the stairs to get breakfast her mother's bedroom door opened and Mrs Brett looked out.

'Diana,' she whispered. 'You were in awfully late last night. I waited up a bit to talk to you, but you were too late for me.'

'I know!' Diana nodded, her blue eyes bright. 'I can't afford too many nights like that. But what was it you wanted?'

'Inspector Pollard was here after you went off with Fenton. The way he was talking, I have the feeling he's going to arrest Geoffrey as soon as he sees him.'

'Really?' Diana frowned. 'Wasn't Geoff at the bungalow last night?'

'There was a policeman on duty there, waiting for Geoffrey to return.'

'I heard a noise over there last night and wondered what it was.' Diana was troubled. 'So they think Geoffrey knows something about Jane Rutherford's disappearance, do they?'

'The Inspector wasn't saying much, but I gather Mrs Rutherford has admitted that Jane was pregnant.'

'Oh Lord! Then the gossip I heard from Alice Reid about Jane and Geoffrey is possibly true.'

'It seems that way! There's always a grain

of truth in even the wildest rumour!' Mrs Brett shook her head sadly. 'My only hope is that Geoffrey hasn't done something foolish.'

'Well Jane *has* disappeared!' Diana went on down the stairs to the kitchen, and her happy thoughts of Fenton were disturbed by the news she had heard from her mother. What had happened to Jane Rutherford? That question must be uppermost in the minds of everyone on St Flavia. But where was Geoffrey? He had been missing since last night! Had he taken fright and fled?

Going into town, Diana found it difficult to keep her mind on her driving. She was concerned about Geoffrey! They had been close friends until Fenton came along, and Geoff had declared love for her. But if he had done something to Jane Rutherford there was not much anyone could do to help him. She drove to the hospital and went in to collect her schedules, and found that she had to fly to Sama, north of St Flavia. Later in the day she had to go on to Tuna, well to the west, and she knew it would be a long, hot day before she saw Fenton again.

Jerry Todd was waiting for her at the quayside, and Diana knew by his expression before he spoke that he had some interesting news to impart. It could only be about the situation surrounding Geoff, she thought as she walked up to him, for Jerry liked his share of gossip.

'Have you heard?' he demanded eagerly. 'The police are looking for Geoff Foster. They think he did away with Jane Rutherford.'

'Did away with her! Have they found her body?' Diana's voice was sharp and filled with surprise.

'No, but it stands to reason that if something drastic hasn't happened to her then she'd be somewhere on the island.'

'I think we'd better be on our way, Jerry, without all this speculation. I don't think all the rumours going the rounds are helping the police much in their search.'

'Foster's motor launch has gone from its moorings, and the police have issued search orders for it. That isn't gossip, Doctor. I was talking to Bill Jennings, the policeman, a few minutes ago. The coastguards will be looking for the boat. It looks as if Foster has run out. Your father is short a manager now.'

'I'm sure that won't worry him as much as the thought that perhaps Geoffrey needs help,' Diana said slowly. 'He must be in serious trouble if he has fled.'

They got into the seaplane and Jerry prepared to take off. He was obviously very much aroused by what was developing in the disappearance of Jane Rutherford, and Diana was worried as they flew towards Sama. She had a cold premonition that they hadn't heard the full story yet about the missing girl, and it seemed to her that Geoff had done something very foolish about Jane and her condition.

After four years as a doctor in the islands, nothing ever surprised Diana any more, but she had to admit to herself that she never thought Geoffrey Foster the kind of man he would have to be to be guilty of what he was suspected. But from what had happened on the beach the night he had watched her and Fenton, she gathered that he was deeper than his character showed, and he was capable of violence.

When they arrived at Sama Diana's work kept her too busy for her thoughts to have much sway, and they didn't leave the island until after lunch. They flew the one hundred and twenty miles to Tuna and landed there, and Diana learned that the rumours concerning Jane Rutherford and Geoffrey Foster had reached this far and were rife around the island. It was popular conjecture that Geoffrey had killed the girl and was now making good his escape, but Diana could not believe that Geoffrey would do such a thing, could not be capable of such violence.

She had to hold a clinic on the island, as well as take care of the patients on her list. She was carrying out a programme of inoculation, and apprehensive children came under her hands and suffered the injections. But Diana's mind was not entirely upon her work, and by the time they were through and could return to St Flavia there was a sense of expectation inside her, a growing dread that shocking disclosures were about to be unleashed upon them. There was a great deal of sympathy in her mind for Geoffrey Foster, and knowing him so well made her feel shocked at the thought he might have murdered a girl.

Jerry Todd was eager to return home, and he talked of nothing but Jane Rutherford all the way. Diana was heartily sick of the subject by the time they sighted St Flavia, and she sighed her relief as the little plane dipped and planed down to meet the waters of the bay.

Inspector Pollard was waiting at the quayside when Diana alighted from the plane, and her heart seemed to miss a beat when she spotted his tall, uniformed figure. Something had happened! She was certain of it as she took her medical bag from Jerry and went towards the policeman. Her tiredness was swept away by a host of other, more vibrant, feelings.

'Doctor, I'm sorry that I have to be here waiting for you at a time like this. I'm sure you must have had a very tiring day.' Inspector Pollard surveyed her flushed face with alert eyes.

'What's happened, Inspector?' The words seemed to stick in Diana's throat. 'Have you caught up with Geoffrey Foster yet?'

'Unfortunately, no! I was hoping you could help me there. Foster has always been a very close friend of yours, hasn't he?'

'He has, but if you think I may know where he's fled then you're going to be disappointed. I have no idea where he may have gone.'

'You visited Sama and Tuna today, didn't you?'

'That's right. There is a lot of talk on both islands about Jane Rutherford's disappearance, but nothing has been seen either of the girl or of Geoffrey Foster.' Diana sighed slowly and heavily. 'What do you think has happened, Inspector?'

'I'm afraid my position does not permit me the luxury of thinking anything, Doctor. I have to go on facts, and they are slowly forthcoming. I know you would help me if you could. You have been instrumental in securing what progress I have already made, but I must ask you to keep your eyes open on your wanderings, and if you see Foster or his motor launch perhaps you'll let me know.'

'I will, Inspector, but I hope all those

rumours are wrong about Geoffrey. It's too horrible to contemplate that he might have done something so very foolish.'

'We must wait and see,' the Inspector told her with serious expression. 'Judgements must wait until the facts are established.' He saluted her and turned away, and Diana walked to her car with deliberate steps, her mind brooding over what she had learned.

She had to take an evening surgery in the town, and did so with growing anticipation. When she was through she telephoned the hospital to learn in advance of her schedules for next day, and learned that she would have to visit Tara and St Lydia.

'But we have weather reports through that aren't too bright,' the clerk in the hospital office informed her. 'There's a bad storm out in the Atlantic and it's coming this way. In some places it's almost at hurricane strength.'

'That sounds exciting.' Diana tried to sound light-hearted, but she knew that storms in this area were never a joke. It was always a problem trying to make emergency calls in such weather, and on some occasions she had lost patients because she had been unable to get to them owing to the weather.

'The storm should be in this area late tomorrow, so perhaps you'll handle a restricted schedule. But we'll know more about it in the morning.'

'Thank you. I'll be in the office at the usual time.' Diana hung up and collected her medical bag. Now she was finished for the day and she could go home!

The thought that Fenton might be there waiting for her filled her with pleasure, and she hurried to her car and set off for the plantation. Night came in slowly as she drove home, and by the time she reached the yard the first stars were twinkling brightly in the velvet sky.

Diana stood in the yard for a moment, staring at Geoffrey's bungalow, and the place seemed desolate without the customary lights at the windows. She wondered about Geoff, a little sad at the way events had gone. But none of them were masters of their Fate, and it was as well that they could not look into the future with any firm knowledge.

There was a breathlessness in the air that warned Diana of what was to come soon, and she suppressed a sigh as she imagined cutting her schedules because of the approaching storm. She tightened her grip upon her bag and turned to the house, and a voice called to her from the nearby shadows. For a moment Diana thought she had imagined the voice, but it came again, low and insistent, filled with vibrant fear, and she was shocked to recognize it as Geoffrey Foster's. For a moment she stood rooted with indecision. Then she put down her bag on the doorstep and turned back in the direction the voice had sounded. She reached the bushes at the side of the house and a hand came out of the shadows and grasped her shoulder.

'Diana, I had to see you!' Foster stood over her, shapeless in the growing night, and the hand he had placed upon her shoulder trembled with nervousness.

'Geoffrey, what on earth are you doing here? Your launch has gone from the harbour. They think you've left the island.'

'That's what I want them to think.' He spoke in low tones, his voice thick and almost unrecognizable.

'What about Jane, Geoffrey?' Diana's lips were stiff as she asked the question. 'What has happened to her?'

'They think I killed her!' His teeth glinted for a moment. 'She's still alive, Diana. I swear it. I took her off the island because she threatened to tell everything if I didn't. I expect you've heard the rumours going around about me, haven't you?'

'I've heard them.' She nodded, suddenly aware that his grip upon her shoulder was hurting. 'Is there any truth in what they are saying?'

'It's true, although I doubt if I am responsible for her condition.' There was bitterness in his voice. 'I went with her! I'm not denying that, but I wasn't the only one.'

'Then why don't you see Inspector Pollard and tell him all about it? If Jane is still alive somewhere then you've got nothing to worry about.'

'Only my future.' He shook his head. 'My job here is finished, Diana, because I'd never be able to face all the sneers and whispers. So I'm getting out now. But I had to see you before I left, knowing the situation that is coming up. I love you, Diana, and I had to make one last effort to get you.'

'Geoffrey, there's so much about this business I just don't understand! Where did you take Jane when she disappeared?'

'She wouldn't want me to say! I've got to go to her shortly and take her on further. She wants to get to South America. I had to fall in with her wishes because she blackmailed me. She threatened to tell the most awful lies about me if I didn't do as she wanted.'

'You haven't killed her, have you, Geoffrey?' Diana was slowly becoming aware of her surroundings. A pang of undefinable emotion began to spread through her. He was holding her tightly, as if afraid that she might suddenly dash away.

He laughed harshly at her question, and his grip tightened upon her shoulder. 'I toyed with the idea that night,' he said slowly. 'God knows why I didn't. She'd been worrying me for days about what she should do. She even came to the bungalow a couple of times, and I was afraid someone in your house would hear her. But I didn't harm her. I took her off the island, and I've left her somewhere where she'll be safe until I can take her the rest of the way. But I didn't bargain for all the trouble her disappearance stirred up. I didn't even care when they suspected Fenton Leigh of knowing something about her disappearance. I even hoped they'd pin something on him because it would take him out of your life. But you're seeing him again, Diana, aren't you?'

'Yes, Geoff. I'm afraid there's nothing you can do about that.' She spoke gently but firmly. 'You are in trouble, I can see that, but you can ease things against yourself by talking to Inspector Pollard. Can't you see that there's nothing against you as far as the law is concerned? This other business will sort itself out in time. But you can't afford to do anything foolish now. You've acted foolishly already by giving in to Jane Rutherford, but a few words will put the matter straight.'

'I'm going away, Diana. I've made up my

mind to that, and I don't want a cloud hanging over my head. I'll take Jane right out of it and no one will know for certain exactly what was wrong with her.'

'Where is she?' Diana could not believe him. If the girl was still alive then he had everything to gain by telling the police what he had done.

'She's waiting on an island. I left her with food and water and shelter, and I shall pick her up shortly. Forget about her. You can tell the police about it yourself, and that should clear up any mystery.'

'Geoff, I can't see you going off like this! You've been such a good manager for my father. You had a good future here! Why throw it all away?'

'When you turned me down the bottom fell out of my world,' he retorted. He lifted his other hand and took hold of her, sliding his arms about her waist, and she tried to hold him at bay as she realized he was going to kiss her.

'This won't help you at all,' she said fiercely. 'Please let me go, Geoffrey!'

'We would have been all right together if Fenton Leigh hadn't come along! He's not right for you, Diana. You'll know only trouble and heartbreak with him.'

Diana struggled silently, trying to break his

grip, and her breath seemed to stick in her throat as he suddenly shifted his grip and lifted his hands to her throat. Panic slashed through her as he exerted his strength.

'You fool!' she gasped. 'You don't know what you're doing!'

'I could kill you to stop him getting you,' he said through his teeth. 'My nerves are at breaking point! I've worked for years to get to the position I held, and my hopes for the future were bright and clear. Then Leigh showed up and mesmerized you! The damned swine! I've lost everything now!'

Diana began to gasp, and she clawed at his hands in desperation, fearing he would strangle her. But he suddenly shook her fiercely and then released her, and Diana fell to the ground and lay gasping. She closed her eyes and her senses spun until she felt dizzy and sick. There were loud sounds in the bushes, then a cry of anger and pain. Opening her eyes, Diana forced herself into a sitting position, and saw two figures struggling in the gloom. There was the sharp sound of a fist striking flesh and one of the figures fell to the ground. The other stood swaying for a moment, then turned and fled, and Diana pushed herself to her feet and leant against a bush, her breath sticking in her throat, her head aching and her neck feeling as if it were broken. She started at the inert figure lying on the ground, and suddenly feared that it might be Fenton. She lurched forward to check, and the figure moved and groaned, then sat up. Diana recognized the Polynesian, Zero.

Still gasping for breath, she helped the native to his feet, and he stood holding his jaw, his teeth white as he grinned.

'Master sent me to watch over you,' he said slowly in passably good English. 'I do poor job!'

'You did all right, Zero,' she told him. 'If you hadn't come along just now I might have been dead.'

'I tell Master. You go into house and wait for him. He come here.'

Before Diana could stop him he had turned and hurried away, and she stood still, listening to the faint sounds of his retreat. When all sounds had faded she took a deep breath and turned to the house, and there were problems in her mind which did not seem to have ready solutions, but she knew she had to ring the Inspector again, and this time, she hoped, would be the last!

The first blast of wind from the approaching storm caught at her as she staggered towards the house, and she almost overbalanced as she fought against it. This seemed to be an omen! The thought crossed her mind as she took up her medical bag. Then she recalled Maria's warning about dangers and difficulties, and she knew that so far the nurse on St Lydia had spoken the truth. It was all coming about. In that illuminating moment Diana felt that the future was far from being assured!

CHAPTER THIRTEEN

Diana called Inspector Pollard and reported her conversation with Geoffrey, but said nothing of his violence towards her. The Inspector asked a lot of questions, but there was very little Diana could tell him beyond the fact that Geoffrey was still on the island. Before presenting herself to her mother, Diana went up to her room, and in her dressing table mirror she examined her reflection, finding dark marks around her throat where Geoffrey had squeezed his fingers. There was a frown upon her lovely face as she thought about Geoffrey, and she wondered how he would make out. She felt no animosity towards him for his attack upon her. He was a deeply passionate man, and his frustrations of the past few days had burdened him intolerably.

She went down to see her mother, and Mrs Brett was full of questions when she heard about the attack on Diana, who tried to play it down. A few moments later there was a heavy knocking at the front door, and Diana went in answer, expecting Fenton, and when she opened the door and saw him standing there, concern in every line of his face, she felt tremendously relieved.

'Are you all right, Diana?' he demanded, crossing the threshold and lifting his hands to her shoulders. 'I met Zero on the ridge and he told me what happened.'

'I'm all right,' she replied. 'But why did you set Zero to watch over me?'

'I didn't like the look of Foster, and after what happened the other night I knew he wasn't to be trusted.' He smiled slowly. 'I had a great advantage over everyone else on the island. I knew for certain that I had nothing to do with that girl's disappearance so I could look in other directions for the man responsible, but everyone thought I was the guilty one. I'm glad now that Zero was around. This could have had an unhappy ending.'

'I never doubted you,' Diana said slowly. 'Fenton, I hope Geoffrey hasn't done anything silly.'

'If he hasn't yet then there's still a chance he will, the way he's beginning to act. But the main thing is, you're all right, Diana.'

'Shaken a little, but all right,' she agreed. 'Come in, Fenton. I haven't been home long, but I was coming to see you later.'

'I've saved you the trouble. I'm sorry but I have to leave St Flavia early in the morning. I'm going back to St Lydia. There was a telephone call from my brother Willard. He wants me to return to the plantation immediately.'

'Anything wrong?' There was concern in her tones, and he smiled gently and patted her arm.

'Now don't you start worrying about that! You're not going to get much fun out of life if you don't learn to relax a little. I told you I have to take my place in the scheme of things, and Willard wants to take a trip. I've got to take care of things while he's away.'

'I'm over on St Lydia at least twice a week,' Diana told him. 'I'll be able to see you, Fenton.'

'Of course you will! But I'm going to miss you, all the same. Can we spend some time together this evening, do you think?'

'Yes. Come and talk with Mother while I get ready. I haven't had time to change yet. But I won't keep you waiting long.'

'Take as long as you like,' he said.

Diana ushered him into her mother's company and left them chatting, and she hurried to get changed. Her weariness dropped from her like a cloak as she went down minutes later to collect him. When they left the house she sighed her relief, and outside in the shadows he took her into his arms and kissed her passionately.

'I would have died if that fool had harmed you,' he whispered. 'But he won't get the chance to touch you again.'

'I think he'll get off the island now,' Diana retorted. 'He won't bother me again.'

'There's no telling with a man like that.' Fenton was uncertain, and worry sounded plainly in his tones.

Diana linked her arm through his, feeling excited by his concern. He kissed her again and they walked along the path towards the ridge.

'When will you arrive at St Lydia tomorrow, Fenton?' She leaned her head against his thick shoulder as they strolled through the shadows. The wind was strengthening, shaking the top branches of the trees about them and Diana shivered and drew closer to him, although the night was warm.

'I should arrive some time in the evening.

There's a storm coming, but it shouldn't be too bad according to the reports. It will probably blow itself out before it reaches us. It usually does in these islands.'

'You'll be careful, won't you?'

'Of course! Don't you worry your pretty head about me. Just take care of yourself, that's all. I don't like the idea of you flying around in that flimsy little seaplane every day.'

'It's far safer up there than on the sea,' she retorted. 'I never have any fears when Jerry is the pilot.'

'All the same, I'd like to see some changes made in your life.' He paused and looked down into her face. 'I suppose there will have to be some changes if we're to continue on this present course, Diana.'

'That's still in the future, but it is worth bearing in mind.'

He kissed her, holding her close, and then they walked on again.

'When will you be at St Lydia?' he demanded. 'Shall I see you over there?'

'I have two stops tomorrow, one at St Lydia and the other at Tara. I could go to Tara first. That will occupy me until noon. Then I could go on to St Lydia, and be there when you arrive.'

'Do that then!' He squeezed her arm. 'I

should have a good wind tomorrow and I'll make fast time. If you don't have to get back too soon we can spend some time together.'

'I'll do it,' she agreed, and they walked on, reaching the ridge and sitting down on a level part to stare down at the lights of the schooner below.

'The sea is getting choppy. Look how the lights are moving. It's going to be a real blow, and no mistake.'

'You'll be careful, won't you?' She reached up and encircled his strong neck with her slender arms. 'I'd die if anything happened to you, Fenton!'

'Nothing is going to happen to me! Our future was planned in Heaven! We have everything to look forward to. We've met, and that was the greatest risk of them all. If Chance had not been on our side we would never have come together in the first place.'

'Do you think so?' His words comforted her and she leaned her head against his shoulder and closed her eyes.

They sat together until it was time for her to go home, and then they walked back down to the house. Standing in its shadow, Fenton kissed her passionately, and told her of his love. She replied similarly, carried away by his fervour, and the night seemed beautifully sympathetic to their passion. As he took his leave he promised to be at St Lydia as early as possible next afternoon, and Diana stood in the doorway and watched him depart. He turned once to wave, and then was gone, and she went into the house slowly, keenly aware that her whole life was wrapped up in him.

She awakened next morning to find the wind shaking the house with its gusting power, but the storm had not materialized as had been expected. She breakfasted and then drove into town to the hospital to learn the situation. She was eager to be on her way, wanting to reach St Lydia and have the chance to spend some time with Fenton.

Thinking of Fenton this morning, she could not prevent her spirits soaring like a bird. She was happy! She had everything to look forward to! Love had made all the difference to her life. She was vibrant with emotion, and she knew her face and eyes proclaimed the fact. But she did not care, and she collected her schedules, informed the clerk that she would be going to Tara in the morning and St Lydia afterwards, and hurried away to the quay.

Parking her car on the quayside, Diana anxiously scanned the bay. The surface was uneasy, showing tiny whitecaps here and there, but it wasn't rough enough to stop them taking off, and relief filled her as she went to the seaplane, where she could see Jerry Todd still busy with an oily rag.

'Are we all set Jerry?' she demanded lightly.

He looked down at her, then dropped to the landing stage at her side. Tiny waves were slapping against the weathered woodwork, setting the whole construction vibrating slightly.

'We're in for some bad weather,' he retorted. 'We could get to Tara all right, but whether we'll be able to go on from there is anybody's guess.'

'We'd better make a start. You know we go on while there's no real danger.'

'The weather can change very quickly,' he pointed out. 'I must say you look very eager this morning. What's been happening to you, Doctor?'

'I'm always keen on my job,' she retorted with a laugh. 'Shall I get aboard?'

'Certainly. We're going, aren't we?' He grinned at her and took her bag, and Diana gave a little sigh of satisfaction as she settled herself in the cockpit. Jerry soon joined her and they strapped themselves in. 'Hold tight,' he commanded. 'Tara, here we come.'

Diana gazed around anxiously as they taxied away from the landing stage, and then Jerry gave the machine full power and they roared into the wind, lifting quickly and soaring like a bird into the high and wide sky. Diana let her pent up breath go in a long sigh, and she smiled at Jerry.

'We're going to be all right today,' he remarked, setting course for Tara. 'This wind will blow us there in no time. But if it gets any stronger we'll be stranded on Tara until the storm abates.'

'I'd rather get stuck on St Lydia, if you can arrange it,' she retorted.

'So that's it, eh?' Jerry smiled at her, nodding. 'Well, I'll see what I can do for you.'

Diana saw that the sea was rough, and she thought of Fenton as they winged their speedy way due south. Tara lay ahead, and to the south-west lay St Lydia. She wished they were about to land on St Lydia, but there was work to do before she could consider her pleasure. She resolutely took her mind from her personal thoughts and began to plan her work routines for when they landed.

The wind had increased considerably by the time they reached Tara, and Diana attended to her duties with increasing fears. She had to get on to St Lydia in order to see Fenton. When she was through she hurried back to the seaplane, and her heart almost failed her when she saw how rough the sea was getting. Jerry grinned at her.

'Looks like we're going to have to stay here,' he said as she reached him.

'No, Jerry! It isn't too rough, is it?'

'Looks very rough, doesn't it?' He stared out across the water. 'I have taken off in rougher weather, but if we delay much longer it will be too rough.'

'What about St Lydia?' she demanded. 'Will it be very rough there for a landing?'

'We'll make it,' he said nonchalantly. 'Get in.'

They took off, and Diana thought they wouldn't get airborne, but Jerry knew what he was doing and they clawed their way into the sky and set course westward. Diana was tense as she stared down at the sea. Out of the shelter of the island the waves were tremendous, and she began to fear that her eagerness had pushed Jerry into making an error of judgement. They still had to land when they reached St Lydia.

But Jerry did not look the least bit concerned as they went on, and forty minutes after leaving Tara they spotted the indistinct mass of St Lydia. Diana looked eagerly for a glimpse of Fenton's ship as they swooped low over the area, and she saw how big the waves were and caught her breath as she looked into Jerry's intent face.

'We can't land there!' He spoke sharply.

'What shall we do?' She relied implicitly upon his judgement, and there was no fear in her as she awaited his reply.

'The lagoon on the other side of the island. It's big enough for us, and this weather won't affect its surface.'

'Of course!' Relief swept through her. 'I'd forgotten all about that.' Diana hunched forward to study the surface of the sea below, and disappointment sped through her when she failed to spot Fenton's schooner.

'Perhaps he had more sense than us and decided not to risk it,' Jerry said, reading her expression and guessing the reason for her concern. 'I heard tell that he was coming back to St Lydia today. But he knew in advance what the weather would be like. Don't worry about him. He knows as much about ships and the sea as I do about planes.'

They skirted the island, the plane shuddering under the stresses applied by the wind. Thick clouds were scudding by high overhead, and Diana knew that when the rain started the tempo of the storm would increase. But they swooped down over the swaying trees and gently kissed the unruffled waters of the lagoon.

'Jerry, while I'm attending to my patients here will you try to find out what happened to Fenton Leigh?' Diana bent her head against the strong wind. 'I'm sure he should have arrived by now.'

'I'll ask around,' the pilot said. 'But we won't be heading back to St Flavia today. You can count on that. This weather is going to get a lot worse.'

Diana nodded and went on her way, but she was worried. She knew Fenton was as eager as she to get here. He would have risked anything for the sake of an evening with her. Had something happened to him out there in the narrow sea between St Lydia and St Flavia? The distance was only fifty-odd miles, and during normal weather there was certainly little danger, but on a day like this anything could happen.

Her fears increased as the wind rose, and by the time she had finished her work she was quivering inside, her imagination filling her with nameless dread. She returned to the Clinic, and sight of Maria, the nurse who had issued her with the warning of dangers and difficulties, brought it all back to mind.

'Has Jerry been here for me, Maria?' she demanded.

'Jerry has gone back to the plane, Doctor!' The nurse's face was taut with concern. 'He said you could join him there.'

'Did he leave any message?' Diana was consumed with impatience.

'He said the ship left St Flavia early this morning and ought to have arrived here about three hours ago. We telephoned St Flavia to check, and Mr. Leigh certainly set sail this morning.'

Diana caught her breath at the words, and a pang speared through her. What could have happened? If Fenton had turned back there would have been word of him. She saw the nurse watching her face intently, and fear made her ask the question which was uppermost in her mind.

'Is this the event you warned me against, Maria?' she demanded. 'You told me I had dangers and difficulties to face.'

'I fear the time has come,' the girl replied hesitantly.

'What can I do?' Diana felt unreality touch the edge of her nerves.

'Nothing! It is beyond our power.'

Diana shook her head and turned away. She went out into the howling wind and hurried back to the lagoon. The trees were protesting against the growing strength of the wind, and the air seemed charged with vibrant anticipation. Jerry Todd was seated behind a couple of steel oil drums, sheltering from the wind, and he looked up at her as she confronted him.

'Have you heard the news about the ship?'

he demanded, and she nodded tiredly. 'What do you reckon has happened? Leigh is a good sailor! He wouldn't make any mistakes. But strange things happen in these seas in a storm.'

'Is there nothing we can do?' She dropped to her knees at his side.

'The sea is very rough out there away from shelter.' He shook his head slowly.

'We could go up and take a quick look around. You've told me this old seaplane can fly in almost any weather.'

'We might get blown away, and the minute we ran out of fuel we'd be dead.' His tones were gentle, but the words were grim. 'Would you risk our lives in a hopeless quest? If we did see them down below we could do nothing about it.'

Diana sighed and shook her head. She didn't like the feeling of helplessness that gripped her. She searched her mind for some hope, no matter how obscure, and knew there was no reason why Fenton should not have returned here on time. Something must have happened to the ship.

'Putting myself in his place,' Jerry said slowly, his eyes upon her taut face, 'I know what I'd do if I was caught out there in the open when the storm came up worse than I expected.'

'What would you do?'

'I'd put into the small natural harbour at Skull Rock. I've heard tell that the natives always put in there when caught unawares by storms. The cleft in the rock which forms the harbour is long enough to take a dozen ships like Leigh's schooner.'

'Fenton has a radio aboard!' Diana's tones rose with excitement. 'Jerry, can you try to raise them?'

'They might be at the bottom of the sea!' Jerry got to his feet. 'But I can try.' He hurried to the seaplane and climbed into the cockpit, and Diana waited tensely. It was a slim chance, but hope flared inside her and she clenched her hands and willed herself not to panic. 'Sorry, I can't raise anything!' Jerry did not look at her as he dropped down beside her. 'It must be the storm. I don't know what to think, Doctor.'

'Would you fly out as far as Skull Rock and take a look around, Jerry?'

'It will be risky. I wouldn't take you if I did!'

'I wouldn't let you go alone! But you know your flying! If you say there's too much danger then I won't ask you again.'

He got to his feet and walked to the edge of the lagoon, pausing to turn slowly, his face inverted to the sky. Diana watched him with unblinking stare, her breath catching in her throat. She had the feeling that they would find Fenton out there, and probably in distress. Jerry came back to her. His face was set in harsh lines.

'It's about twenty-five miles to Skull Rock,' he said slowly. 'That's fifteen minutes flying time. I reckon we could make it with little trouble. I have flown in this sort of weather before, and so have you, but only where there has been a life at stake. This could be a wild goose chase.'

'We'll have to attempt it, Jerry,' she said firmly.

'Then what are we waiting for? The longer we delay the worse the weather will be. It hasn't started to blow yet! But we will have time to make one pass around Skull Rock, Doctor. If we don't see anything that first time we come straight back here.'

'Agreed!' Diana patted his arm. 'Thank you, Jerry.'

'I wouldn't do it for anyone else,' he retorted with a grin.

They got into the plane and he taxied to the end of the lagoon, turning slowly and preparing for take-off. Diana sat tensely in her seat, clenching her hands, and it seemed to her that events were taking control of them. She had a strange, uncanny feeling in her mind that they were just acting out the parts that Fate intended, and when the plane rose in the air like a startled bird and shivered in the merciless grip of the wind she closed her eyes for a moment and prayed.

Jerry set course and held the machine steady. Diana was shocked when she saw the size of the waves off the island. She glanced at Jerry and he grinned at her, his face showing confidence.

'It always looks worse from up here,' he said tersely.

Diana nodded and sat on the edge of her seat as the minutes ticked away. In no time at all they were swaying into a turn, and there below them lay the desolate Skull Rock. Spray was leaping up the sheer walls of the rock as the storm threw wave after wave at the base. The trees on the top of the rock containing the ruined temple were quivering under the onslaughts of the wind. The whole area looked wild and desolate, brooding and foreboding, and Diana stifled a shudder as she bent sideways and peered down at the place.

The next moment they were sweeping across the cleft that formed a long, narrow harbour stretching almost across the whole length of the high island, and Jerry uttered a shout as he saw something down there which didn't belong. He banked steeply and the wind tore at them, thrusting with invisible power at them, making the controls difficult to handle, and Diana froze in her seat as she made out the shape of a ship safely at anchor in the calm water amid the storm.

'It's down there!' she cried. 'That was Fenton's ship! I recognized it.'

'I guessed he would have sense enough to fetch up in there.' Jerry grinned. He glanced at her, his face gentle for a moment. 'Now we'd better get out of here or they'll have to come looking for us. We're going back to St Lydia.'

Before Diana could answer there was a jarring sensation in the plane, and they both looked around quickly. To Diana's horror she saw fabric stripping itself from the wingtip of the plane, and Jerry uttered a shout of despair when he spotted it. She saw him clench his teeth, and the next instant he had banked the machine and was heading back the way they had come, making for the cleft in Skull Rock.

'What are you going to do?' she demanded shrilly.

'We're going to have to set down, Doctor. That wing will be stripped completely in a matter of moments.'

'You're going down into that space where the ship is?' she demanded in fear.

'Would you rather go down in the open

sea?' he retorted, his eyes narrowed as he stared ahead.

Diana caught her breath as he swung slightly. They were over the open sea and approaching the narrow cleft. Huge waves were boiling up at the entrance to the cleft, but just beyond she could see the smooth water where the ship was anchored. To her worried eyes it seemed that the distance in which they had to put down was not nearly long enough, but she trusted Jerry, and fear mounted in her as he went as low as he dared to the great, breaking waves.

Spray lashed at them as they flew into the cleft, and turbulence threatened to send them spinning down into the broiling water. But Jerry fought the controls and they passed through the turmoil, their floats striking calmer water almost at the point where the waves thinned out. Jerry hunched forward, eyes on the opposite wall of rock, and Diana clenched her teeth and her hands and waited for the inevitable crash.

She saw the outline of Fenton's schooner rapidly drawing nearer, and there was a prayer of relief on her lips when she saw that the ship would not bar their landing. They skimmed alongside, and then there was another craft in front of them, almost at the end of their run-in. Jerry shouted a warning and Diana tensed herself. They were not travelling fast now, and slowing with each succeeding yard, and then came the shattering impact.

Diana was thrown forward against her safety strap, but that did not prevent her forehead striking the panel in front of her. She felt the impact, but strangely enough there was no pain. Her vision failed her suddenly and she slumped into unconsciousness, faintly aware of the shuddering and the crackling sounds of the plane breaking up. Then she knew no more...

She came back to consciousness very slowly, like a swimmer breaking surface after a particularly deep dive, and the first thing she saw was Fenton's worried face bending over her. She looked around in wonder and saw that she was on the bunk in his cabin, and Jerry was sitting nearby at the table, grinning when he saw her movements.

'Fenton!' She could not believe this was no dream! Perhaps they had all perished and this was after death! 'What happened?' Her hand lifted to her forehead and she felt the painful swelling where she had made contact with the plane. 'Are you all right?' she demanded.

'She almost gets killed herself, and the first thing she asks is are you all right!' Jerry spoke cheerfully, and he got to his feet and came across to stand at Fenton's side, peering down into her face with worry showing upon his own. 'Perhaps I'd better leave you two alone,' Jerry continued. 'All I've got to say, Doctor, is that we're both very lucky to be alive. The plane is finished though. It's at the bottom of the cleft now, where we would have been if Mr Leigh and his crew hadn't pulled us out.'

Diana looked up into Fenton's face, and Jerry turned and climbed out of the cabin.

'You shouldn't have come after me, Diana,' Fenton said slowly. 'We saw you going over, and I guessed you were worried about us.'

'I would rather have perished out here than lived on if anything had happened to you,' she said. 'What delayed you? You should have been in St Lydia long before the storm got this bad.'

'We were passing here when I spotted movement on the top.' Fenton's face was expressionless. 'I decided to put in and investigate, and spotted Geoffrey Foster's launch. You hit it when you landed, by the way. The movement on the top of the cliff was Jane Rutherford, trying to attract our attention. Foster brought her out here the day she disappeared from St Flavia, and he came back in the night to pick her up, so she tells me. But he slipped on the rocks and broke a leg. I've fixed him up, and we're going to have to wait here for the storm to abate before we can go on. I couldn't radio the situation to the police, or anyone, because we're land-locked here and the set won't work.'

Diana shook her head as she listened, and her mind seemed to teeter with relief. Now the dangers and the difficulties were past, she was certain, and when Fenton took her gently into his arms and kissed her she knew nothing could affect their future.

'I have the feeling that we're going to be stuck in here for quite some time, Diana,' he said, kissing her gently. 'But we need time to ourselves, don't we? I don't think we've spent more than a couple of hours together at any one time since we met.'

'We can soon remedy that,' she retorted, sitting up and putting her arms around his neck. 'Fenton, I'm sure no one is going to hold anything of the past against you when we get in with Jane Rutherford and Geoffrey. You've proved yourself enough for anyone.'

'You're the only one I care about,' he retorted softly. 'So long as you're satisfied with me then it doesn't matter about all the rest.'

'I'm satisfied,' she said. 'But what about me? Are you happy with me?'

He made no reply, but studied her face intently for a moment. Then he kissed her with all the power he could muster, and

Diana found her answer in his lips. Outside the cleft the storm raged on in mounting fury but nothing it could do equalled the power of their love, for Diana had overcome the storm itself to be at his side, and that was where she wanted to remain for the rest of her life. His arms were a safe haven, his love a perfect gift. Time lost all meaning as they waited out the storm, and time itself was on their side . . .

The publishers hope that this book has given you enjoyable reading. Large Print Books are specially designed to be as easy to see and hold as possible. If you wish a complete list of our books, please ask at your local library or write directly to: Curley Publishing, Inc., P.O. Box 37, South Yarmouth, Massachusetts, 02664.